MAXIMUM RIDE:

THE FINAL WARNING

James Patterson

GALAXY

PLUS

First published in Great Britain in
2008
by Headline Book Publishing
a division of Hodder Headline
This Large Print edition published
by
BBC Audiobooks 2009
by arrangement with
Headline Book Publishing

ISBN: 978 1405 663618

British Library Cataloguing in Publication Data available

Printed and bound in Great Britain by
CPI Antony Rowe, Chippenham, Wiltshire

For Andrea and Lucy
The flock grows and prospers;
all is well, all is good

Many thanks to Gabrielle Charbonnet, my
conspirator, who flies high and cracks wise.
And to Mary Jordan,
for brave assistance and research at every
twist and turn.

To the Reader:

The idea for the Maximum Ride series comes from earlier books of mine called *When the Wind Blows* and *The Lake House*, which also feature a character named Max who escapes from a quite despicable School. Most of the similarities end there. Max and the other kids in the Maximum Ride books are not the same Max and kids featured in those two books. Nor do Frannie and Kit play any part in the series. I hope you enjoy the ride anyway.

Prologue

CATCHING BIRD FREAKS: HAZARDOUS DUTY AT BEST

CHAPTER ONE

Windsor State Forest, Massachusetts

Sssss.

The soldiers' armor made an odd hissing noise. But besides the slight sound of metal plates sliding smoothly, flawlessly over one another, the troop was unnaturally quiet as it moved through the woods, getting closer to the prey.

The faintest of beeps caused the team leader to glance down at his wrist screen. Large red letters scrolled across it: ATTACK IN 12 SECONDS . . . 11 . . . 10 . . .

The team leader tapped a button, and the screen's image changed: a tall, thin girl with dirt smears on her face and a tangle of brown hair, glaring out at him. TARGET 1 was superimposed on her face.

. . . 9 . . . 8 . . .

His wrist screen beeped again, and the image changed to that of a dark-haired, dark-eyed, scowling boy. TARGET 2.

And so on, the image changing every half second, ending finally with a portrait of a small, scruffy black dog looking at the camera in surprise.

The team leader didn't understand why

Target 7 was an animal. He didn't need to understand. All he needed to know was that these targets were slated for capture.

...3...2...1...

The leader emitted a whistle pitched so high that only his team members could hear it. He motioned toward the small run-down cabin they had surrounded in the woods.

Synchronized perfectly, as only machines can be, the eight team members shouldered eight portable rocket launchers and aimed them straight at the cabin. With a *whoosh*, eight large nets made of woven Kevlar strands shot out from the cannons and unfolded with geometric precision in midair, encasing the cabin almost entirely.

The team leader smiled in triumph.

CHAPTER TWO

'The prey have been captured, sir,' the team leader said in a monotone. Pride was not tolerated in this organization.

'Why do you say that?' the Uber-Director asked in a silky tone.

'The cabin has been secured.'

'No. Not quite,' said the Uber-Director, who was little more than a human head attached by means of an artificial spinal

4

column to a series of Plexiglas boxes. The bioengine that controlled the airflow over his vocal cords allowed him to sigh, and he did. 'The chimney. The skylight.'

The team leader frowned. 'The chimney would be impossible to climb,' he said, accessing his internal encyclopedia. Photographs of the prey scrolled quickly across the team leader's screen. Suddenly an important detail caught his attention, and he froze.

In the corner of one of the photographs, a large feathered wing was visible. The team leader tracked it, zooming in on just that section of the image. The wing appeared to be attached to the prey.

The prey could fly.

He had left routes of escape open.

He had failed!

The Uber-Director closed his eyes, sending a thought signal to the nanoprocessors implanted in his brain. He opened his eyes in time to see the team leader and his troop vaporize with a crackling, sparking fizzle. All that was left of them was a nose-wrinkling odor of charred flesh and machine oil.

Part One

ANOTHER PART OF THE BIG PICTURE

CHAPTER THREE

A different forest. Not telling you where.

Okay, it doesn't take a genius to figure out that funerals suck. Even if you didn't know the person, it's still totally sad. When you did know the person, well, let's just say it's much worse than broken ribs. And when you just found out that the person was your biological half brother, right before he died, it adds a whole new level of pain.

Ari. My half brother. We shared the same 'father,' Jeb Batchelder, and you can believe those quotes around 'father.'

I'd first known Ari as a cute little kid who used to follow me around the School, the horrible prison–science facility where I grew up. Then we'd escaped from the School, with Jeb's help, and to tell you the truth, I hadn't given Ari another thought.

Then he'd turned up Eraserfied, a grotesque half human, half wolf, his seven-year-old emotions all askew inside his chemically enhanced, genetically modified brain. He'd been turned into a monster, and they'd sent him after us, with various unpredictable, gruesome results.

Then there had been that fight in the subway tunnels beneath Manhattan. I'd whacked Ari's head a certain way, his neck had cracked against the platform's edge . . . and suddenly he'd been dead. For a while, anyway.

Back when I thought I had killed him, all sorts of sticky emotions gummed up my brain. Guilt, shock, regret . . . but also relief. When he was alive, he kept trying to kill us—the flock, I mean. Me and my merry band of mutant bird kids. So if he was dead, that was one less enemy gunning for my family.

All the same, I felt horrible that I had killed someone, even by accident. I'm just tenderhearted that way, I guess. It's hard enough being a homeless fourteen-year-old with, yeah, *wings*, without having a bunch of damp emotions floating all over the place.

Now Ari was dead for real. I hadn't killed him this time, though.

'I need a tissue.' Total, our dog, sniffled, nuzzling around my ankles like I had one in my sneakers.

Speaking of damp emotions.

Nudge pressed closer to me and took my hand. Her other hand was over her mouth. Her big brown eyes were full of tears.

None of us are big criers, not even six-year-old Angel, or the Gasman, who's still only eight. Nudge is eleven, and Iggy, Fang, and I are fourteen. *Technically*, we're all still children.

But it takes a lot, and I mean a whole lot, to

make any of us cry. We've had bones broken without crying about it. Today, though, it was like another flood was coming, and Noah was building an ark. My throat hurt so much from holding back tears that it felt as though I'd swallowed a fist of clay.

Angel stepped forward and gently tossed a handful of dirt onto the plain wooden box at the bottom of the big hole. A hole it had taken all of us three hours to dig.

'Bye, Ari,' she said. 'I didn't know you for very long, and I didn't like you for a lot of it. But I liked you at the end. You helped us. You saved us. I'll miss you. And I didn't mind your fangs or anything.' Her little voice choked, and she turned to bury her face against my chest.

I stroked her hair and swallowed hard.

The Gasman was next. He too sprinkled dirt on the coffin. 'I'm sorry about what they did to you,' he said quietly. His spiky blond hair caught a shaft of sunlight and seemed to light up this little glen. 'It wasn't your fault.'

I snuck a quick glance over at Jeb. His jaw was clenched, his eyes full of pain. His only son lay in a box in the ground. He had helped put him there.

Bravely, Nudge stepped closer to the grave and tossed some dirt onto it. She tried to speak but started crying. I drew her to me and held her close.

I looked at Iggy. As if sensing it, he raised

11

his hand and dropped it. 'I don't have anything to say.' His voice was gruff.

Next it was Fang's turn, but he waved me to go. Total had collapsed in sobs on my shoes, so I gently disengaged him and stepped over to the grave. I had two hothouse lilies, and I let them float onto the coffin of my half brother.

As the flock leader, I was supposed to come up with a speech. There was no way to sum up what I was feeling. I had killed Ari once, then watched him die again as he saved my life. I'd known him when he was a cute little kid, and I'd known him as a hulking Eraser. I had fought him almost to death, and I had ended up choosing him over the best friend I'd ever had. I'd hated everything about him, then found out we shared half of our human DNA.

I had no words for this, and I'm a word *queen*. I've talked my way out of more tight spots than a leopard has, but this? A funeral for a sad, doomed seven-year-old? I had nothing.

Fang came up behind me and touched my back. I looked at him, at his dark eyes that gave away nothing. He nodded and sort of patted my hair, then moved forward and dropped some dirt onto the coffin.

'Well, Ari, I'm sorry that it's ended like this,' he said so quietly I could hardly hear him, even with my raptor super-hearing. 'You were a decent little kid, and then you were a total nightmare. I didn't trust you—until the very end. I didn't know you much, didn't care to.' Fang stopped and brushed some overlong hair out of his eyes. 'Right now, that feels like the biggest tragedy of all.'

Okay, that so did me in. Mr. Rock being all emotional? Expressing feelings? Tears spilled down my cheeks, and I covered my mouth with my hand, trying not to make a sound. Nudge put her arm around me, feeling my shoulders shaking, and Angel held me tight. Then everyone was holding me, total flock hug, and I put my head on Fang's shoulder and cried.

CHAPTER FOUR

There's no rest for the wicked. But you knew that.

As soon as the sob-fest was over and Ari was buried, Jeb said, 'We need to go.' His face was pale and unhappy. 'Dr. Martinez and I talked to you about this trip to Washington. We think it's crucial that you guys attend this meeting.' He sighed, not looking at Ari's grave.

'Why is this important, again?' I asked, trying to turn my back on feeling sad. Not so easy. 'You said something about government, blah blah blah?'

Jeb began to head out of the woods. With me in the lead and Fang taking up the rear, we followed him cautiously.

'After everything that happened in Germany,' Jeb said, 'we were contacted by some very important higher-ups in the government. People who understand, who are on our side.'

I felt like saying, 'What's this "our side," kemosabe?' but didn't.

'They're eager to meet with you,' he went on. 'Frankly, these would be important and valuable allies—people who could actually offer you protection and resources. But they're very hands-on—they need to see the miracle kids with their own eyes.' He turned back and gave us a rueful smile.

'If by "miracle kids" you mean innocent test-tube babies whose DNA was forcibly unraveled and merged with two percent avian genes, yeah, I guess that would be us,' I said. 'Because it's a miracle that we're not complete *nut jobs* and mutant *disasters.*'

Jeb winced and gave a brief nod, accepting his role in our short, hard lives. 'Well, as I said, they're eager to see you. And your mom— Dr. Martinez—and I really recommend you go.' We came to the edge of the woods, and there was a small landing strip, scraped into the forest like a wound. A sleek private jet waited there, two armed Secret Service agents

14

standing at the entry stairs.

I halted about ten yards away, doing a quick recon. Force of habit. No one started shooting at us. No hordes of Erasers or Flyboys swarmed out of the woods.

'I don't know,' I said, looking at the jet. 'It feels weird that no one's throwing a black hood over my head.'

Fang smirked next to me.

Jeb had walked on ahead, and now he turned. 'Max, we talked about this. This jet will actually get you to Washington faster than you can fly yourselves.'

Are we junior pilots? you ask. Why, no. If there are a couple of new readers out there, welcome! That mutant thing I mentioned? We're 98 percent human, 2 percent bird. We have wings; we fly. Keep reading. You'll get it all soon.

'Yeah,' I said, still feeling doubtful. Mostly I just wanted to turn, run, and throw myself into the air. That sweet rush of freedom, feeling my powerful wings lift me off the ground . . .

Instead, Jeb wanted to pack me into a little jet, like a sardine. A sullen, feathery sardine.

'Max,' Jeb said more softly, and I automatically went on guard. 'Don't you trust me?'

Six pairs of flock eyes turned toward him. Seven, if you counted Total.

I mentally reviewed possible responses:

15

1) Sardonic laughter (always good)
2) Rolled eyes and snort of disbelief
3) Sarcastic 'You have *got* to be kidding me.'

Any of those responses would have been fine. But lately I had grown up a bit. A little heartbreak, a little fighting to the death, finding out who my real parents were—it all aged a girl.

So instead I looked at Jeb and said evenly, 'No. But I trust my mother, and she apparently trusts you. So, little tin-can jet it is.'

I walked steadily toward the plane, seeing the glimpse of pain and regret in Jeb's eyes. Would I ever be able to forgive him for all the heinous things he had done to me, to the flock? He'd had his reasons; he'd thought he was helping, thought it was for the greater good, thought it would help me in my mission.

Well, la-di-dah for him. I don't forgive that easy.

And I *never, ever* forget.

CHAPTER FIVE

The jet didn't have normal rows of seats. It looked more like a living room inside, with couches and easy chairs and coffee tables.

There were more Secret Service agents here, and to tell you the truth, they gave me the creeps—even though I knew they were the same people who sometimes protected the president. But there's something about plain black suits, sunglasses, and little headsets that just automatically makes me twitchy.

Combine that with the inevitable heart-pounding claustrophobia that came from being enclosed in a small space, and I was basically ready to shred anyone who talked to me.

On the other hand, if anything dicey happened to the plane, I knew six flying kids who would come out okay.

I did a quick 360 of the plane's interior. Angel and Total were curled up on a small couch, asleep. The Gasman and Fang were playing poker, using pennies as chips. Iggy was sprawled in a lounger, listening to the iPod my mom had given him.

'I'm Kevin Okun, your steward. Would you like a soda?' A very handsome man holding drinks stopped by my chair.

Don't mind if I do, Kevin Okun. 'Uh, a Diet Coke? One that hasn't been opened yet.' *Can't be too careful.*

He handed me a sealed can and a plastic cup of ice. Across from me, Nudge sat up eagerly. 'Do you have Barq's? It's root beer. I had it in New Orleans, and it's fabulous.'

'I'm sorry—no Barq's,' said Kevin Okun,

our steward.

'Okay,' said Nudge, disappointed. 'Do you have any Jolt?'

'Well, that has a lot of caffeine,' he said.

I looked at Nudge. 'Yeah, because after everything we've been through, we're worried about your caffeine intake.'

She grinned, her smooth tan face lighting up.

The steward put the drink on the little table between me and Nudge.

'Thank you,' Nudge said. The steward headed back to the galley, and Nudge reached for the can.

When her hand was still a couple of inches away, the can slid toward her fingers, and she grabbed it.

Instantly we looked at each other.

'The plane tilted,' she said.

'Yeah, of course,' I agreed. 'But . . . just to see, just for our own amusement, let's . . .' I took the can away from her and put it back on the table. I reached for it. It stayed put.

Nudge reached for it.

It slid toward her.

Our eyes wide, we stared at each other.

'The plane tilted again,' Nudge said.

'Hm,' I said. I took the can away and had her come at it from a different angle. The can slid toward her.

'I'm *magnetic,*' she whispered, half awed and

half horrified.

'I hope you don't start sticking to fridges and stuff,' I said in disbelief.

Fang dropped down next to me, and the Gasman joined us, squishing in next to Nudge.

'What's going on?' Fang asked.

'I'm Magnet Girl!' Nudge said, already coming to terms with her new skill.

Eyebrows raised, Fang picked up a metal pen and held it against Nudge's arm. He let go, and it dropped to the floor.

Nudge frowned. Then she reached down for the pen, and it flew into her hand from a few inches away.

Gazzy gave a low whistle. 'You're *kind of* magnetic. Cool!'

'No, that's not it,' said Fang quietly. 'It's that you can *attract* metal—maybe only when you want to.'

Well. The rest of the flight zipped by as we played with Nudge's bizarre newfound ability. When we got close to DC, Jeb came over to give us a ten-minute heads-up. One glance at our faces and his eyes narrowed.

'What's going on?' It was the same dad-like, no-nonsense tone that he had used years ago, when it was just us and him in our secret house in the Colorado mountains. He'd made that exact face the day he found the frogs in the toilet. I remembered it so clearly, but it seemed like three lifetimes ago.

Before I could say, 'Nothing,' Nudge blurted, 'I can make metal come to me!'

Jeb sat down, and Nudge demonstrated.

'I don't know why you can do that,' he said slowly. 'As far as I know, it was never programmed in.' He looked around at all of us. 'It's possible . . . It's possible that maybe you guys are starting to mutate on your own.'

CHAPTER SIX

You are reading Fang's Blog. Welcome!
You are visitor number: 4,792

Whatever the tally counter at the top tells you, your number is actually way higher than that. Our counter thing broke, and we finally got it working again. But it started again at zero. Anyway, thanks for checking in.

We're all okay, but we just buried a friend. I know some of you out there have lost someone close to you, and now I get a little bit of what it's like. The guy who died—I knew him for a long time, but not that well, and for the past six months, I've hated his guts. Then I suddenly didn't. Then he died.

For me what was harder than losing him was watching what it did to people around me. The one thing I really can't stand is when Max and the others are in pain or upset. Not upset like in angry or teed off, 'cause God knows if that got to me I'd be totally out of luck. But upset like in crying, sadness, regret—all that stuff. I hate it. It kills me. I know what it takes to make these kids cry, to make Max cry, and I hate that they had to go through that.

But enough of all that emo stuff. The end result is: We're all good. We're all alive. I'm glad about that, about the six of us. They're who matter to me. Even when Max is being a pigheaded, stubborn idiot dictator, she's still the one I want by my side. Though I can feel myself getting ulcers and gray hairs from dealing with her.

Anyway! We're on our way to a hush-hush meeting with some top-secret bigwigs, ooh. Yep, fighting to the death one day, drinking frosty little drinks on a private jet the next. It's enough to make anyone schizo.

I don't have too much else to say right now, so I'll answer some questions that you guys have sent in.

Dylan from Omaha writes:
Its so cool that you guys can fly. Do you have any other superpowers?

Well, Dylan, yes we do. Iggy is a crack

accountant, as long as someone reads him the numbers. And Gazzy can whip up a lemon meringue pie like nobody's business.

No, seriously, we may have a couple tricks up our wings, but we're not gonna tell you or anyone else. The more that people know about us, the more ways they can think up to mess with us. Capiche? Nothing personal.
— Fang

Sweetmarie420 from Gainesville writes:
When you guyz grow up, will you lay eggz or have babeez♥?

With any luck at all, I won't do either. Not sure about Max, Nudge, and Angel. Don't wanna find out anytime soon.
— Fang

Zeroland from Tupelo writes:
I wish ida been there at your big battle, man. It woulda been so awesome!!!!

Kid, you need another definition for awesome. You don't want to be anywhere near one of our battles. *I* don't even want to be near our battles. Unfortunately, the evil idiots usually don't give me a choice.
— Fang

MelysaB from Boulder writes:

22

I know you have to hide out sometimes. I'm a guide in the Colorado mountains around Boulder, and I could help you find some good hiding places.

Thanks, MelysaB. We love the Colorado mountains. And we're never gonna take you up on your offer. If you're one of Them, then this is a trap. If you're not one of Them, then doing anything for us puts you in danger. But thanks anyway.
— Fang

Okay, gotta go. Peace out.
— Fang

CHAPTER SEVEN

It had been only a few days since I'd seen Dr. Martinez—aka Mom—but it was great seeing her again.

Ella, my half sister, was back home in Arizona, but Mom had come to DC to be with us at our big meeting. We hugged for a long time, then she hugged the rest of the flock, who ate it up. Total coughed meaningfully at her feet, and she leaned down and hugged him too.

Mom and Jeb took us to a safe house where

23

we could rest up before the meeting. To us, the words *safe house* have about as much meaning as *jumbo shrimp.* No house would ever feel safe enough. Maybe if it were on Mars, and we could see rockets coming from thousands of miles away . . .

After a fabulous hot shower, I got into clean clothes and untangled my hair. It was getting longer, after being cut pretty short in New York, months ago. I looked at myself in the mirror and, bonus, didn't see an Eraser looking out at me with my eyes. This had happened to me a couple times in the past, completely freaking me out.

I didn't look like a little kid anymore. I looked older, like a teenager.

'What are you doing in there, waxing your mustache?' Iggy yelled, pounding on the bathroom door.

I yanked the door open and pushed him backward hard, making him stagger. 'I don't have a mustache, you idiot!' Iggy giggled and put his arms up to protect himself in case I punched him. 'And you know what?' I added. 'You don't have one either. Well, maybe in a couple years. You can always hope.'

I left him in the hallway, anxiously fingering his upper lip.

In the living room, the rest of the flock sat around looking uncomfortable and unnaturally clean. As soon as I appeared, Total trotted over to me, his fur glossy.

'I got *bathed!*' he grumbled.

'You look lovely,' I said with a straight face. I patted his back. 'You're all fluffy and soft.' I left him while he was deciding whether to be appalled or flattered.

Fang was standing by a front window, gazing out from behind a privacy curtain.

'Anything going on out there?' I asked.

He flicked a glance at me, shook his head, then took a longer look. 'What happened to your tan?'

'It was dirt.'

He grinned, one of his rare grins that make the world spin a little faster. As if he didn't know what he was doing, he reached out and touched my hair where it lay on my shoulders. 'You look . . . like a girl.' His voice held bemusement.

'There's a reason for that,' I said seriously.

'No, I mean like a real—' He seemed to catch himself, shook his head, and looked back out the window.

I crossed my arms. 'Like a real what?' *Watch your step here, Fang,* I thought, *or I'll flatten you.*

While he hesitated, Nudge came up. 'Ooh, Max, you look great!' she said, admiring my clothes. 'That top is totally hot! You look like you're at least sixteen!'

'Thanks,' I muttered, now feeling

25

embarrassed. Since my usual attire is ancient and usually bloodstained T-shirts and jeans, I guess I did look a little different.

Okay, Max.

My eyes flickered when I heard the Voice inside my head. (You mean you don't have one? You can get 'em at Target.)

This meeting is very important, so no funny business. Just remember your mission, keep your mind open, and listen to what they have to say.

Yeah, whatever, Jeb, I thought. *Save the world, yada, yada, yada. You can go now.*

I'm not Jeb, said the Voice. *You were wrong about that.*

Huh? I thought blankly.

You have part of the picture, Max, said the Voice. *Not all of the picture. Sometimes when you're at your most certain, that's when everything you know is wrong.*

Oh, God, not again. I wanted to scream. My whole life was taking two steps forward and one step back. Would I ever just get ahead?

You're making progress, the Voice assured me. *You're a couple steps ahead.*

Just then Jeb came into the room. He rubbed his hands together as if he were cold. 'Time to go, kids.'

CHAPTER EIGHT

You've all seen the Capitol Building in Washington DC, like on postcards, right? It's the big white one with the dome on top that isn't the White House. Anyway, it's gigundo. We drove up in our black limousine, feeling like celebrities. Inside we were led through a series of hallways and stairs until we were in a large conference room with a great view of some gardens.

In the conference room, about twenty people sat around a big wooden table. Some of the people were in military uniforms. Everyone sat up and turned to stare at us when we came in, surrounded by Secret Service agents. I didn't even know I wanted to hold someone's hand until Mom laced her fingers in mine and gave a squeeze. Suddenly it all seemed better.

'Welcome. Thank you for coming.' A tall man in an olive green uniform came forward and solemnly shook hands with Jeb, then Mom, then all of us kids. 'Please sit down. Would you care for something to drink? We have coffee, tea, soda, ice water . . . Oh, and I see you brought your dog. A cute little Scottie.' He smiled uncertainly, as if wondering why someone had let an animal into the building. I bit my lip, wondering if Total was going to mouth off. But he didn't. He just seethed quietly and hopped up onto his own chair by Angel's.

The next hour was like, 'This is your life, mutant bird kids!' They didn't have any pictures or film of us when we were little and still living in dog crates at the School. But the past six months were decently documented. They had films of us flying, way overhead, and footage of various fights with people, Erasers, and the latest heinous incarnation of enemies, the Flyboys. There was some footage of us just chilling at Anne Walker's house in northern Virginia. It made me tense up and get mad all over again.

Last, there were about three minutes of choppy, grainy film that had been shot inside Itex's picturesque German headquarters. It showed me squaring off against Omega, poster boy for pathetic losers. It showed the riot that some of the clones had started, and the crowd of angry kids breaking through the castle wall.

It showed Ari dying.

The film stopped, and the dimmed lights brightened. Shades lifted automatically, revealing the large windows again.

Now I was in a totally rotten mood. It was bad enough that I was all dressed up like some fashion geek, but I'd managed to not think about Ari for about five minutes, and then I had to watch him die all over again. I snuck a glance at Jeb, who was white faced, one hand clenched tightly around a pencil as he stared at the table.

'You six are most impressive.' A woman in a tailored gray skirt-suit stood up and poured herself a glass of water. She smiled at us, but it was the kind of smile that didn't reach her eyes.

'We've asked you to come here today because we're very interested in your future,' said an older man. 'We—the American government, that is—didn't know of your existence until quite recently. Now that we know, we want to protect you and also explore whether we can be useful to each other.'

They were certainly putting their cards on the table. Usually there was a lot of mumbo jumbo about how special and unique we were, et cetera, but what they were always really getting at was: Can we make you do what we want you to?

So far the answer had always been 'Nope!'

The man paused, looking at us one by one, as if waiting for a response. He got none.

'One way *we* could be useful to *you* would be for us to create a school, a place where you could live safely.' A younger blond woman was talking to us, but clearly her words were aimed at Jeb and my mom. Like they made decisions for us or something. 'You're very gifted at

29

survival, but there are significant gaps in your education. We could fill in those gaps, help you realize your full potential.'

Again there was a pause while the government people waited for us to jump up and down with excitement over the idea of going to school. *School* was, of course, an unfortunate word choice on their part.

'To what end?' My voice was clear, no wavering.

'Excuse me?' The younger woman looked at me.

'What would you guys get out of it?' I asked. 'Besides the sheer joy of helping us fulfill our potential.'

'We would get to study you, frankly,' said a tall, lean man who, I kid you not, looked just like Bill Nye the Science Guy. 'You're like nothing we've ever seen before. The idea that human children can actually fly is mind-blowing. While you're at the school, we could study you, understand the physical changes that enable you to fly.'

'To what end?' I asked again. 'So that you can make more of us?'

The man looked genuinely surprised. 'No,' he said. 'Just to . . . understand.'

I decided I liked him. Too bad he was one of Them.

'Okay, say you get to study us,' I said agreeably. 'Somehow you get us to believe that it wouldn't be a *complete nightmare* for us to be hooked up to sensors while we run on treadmills, or to hold our own in wind tunnels while you film us flying. Then what?'

Silence.

CHAPTER NINE

An older man with the collar stars of a general spoke next. 'What do you mean?'

'I mean, what *else?*' I said. 'You study us; you get the warm fuzzies from helping us with all that potential we have lying around. What else do you want from us?'

The general's blue eyes were cold and intelligent in a ruddy, grandfatherly face.

'What makes you think there would be something else?' he asked.

'Um, because I'm not a complete moron?' I offered. 'Because no grown-up has ever been completely straight with us? Because I don't believe for one second that you're giving us the whole story. I don't believe for *one second* that all you want is to study us. You know and I know that you've got ulterior motives up that crisply starched sleeve. The only question is, when are you gonna show us what they are?'

The government people all seemed taken aback. It was kind of sad, how universally grown-ups seemed surprised when kids didn't unquestioningly fall into line. I mean, what kind of kids were they used to dealing with?

I waited a minute while they regrouped. My mom squeezed my hand under the table. One by one I quickly met the flock's eyes: Fang's were alert, Iggy's were leveled directly at me, Nudge's were wide and trusting. The Gasman's were full of mischief, and I had a moment's worry before I realized he probably couldn't have snuck any explosives into this building. Angel was watching me calmly, and now she gave me a little smile. Total put his paws on the table and drank noisily from a glass of water. People looked at him, horrified, and I almost cracked up.

'Any other questions?' I asked, deciding it was time to wrap up this sideshow.

'Why wouldn't you want our protection?' a woman asked, seeming truly baffled. I guessed she hadn't been working there too long.

'Because it comes with a price, with strings,' I explained. 'The price is too high, and the strings are too tight.'

'You're children,' said a middle-aged man in a blue suit. 'Don't you want a home, a family?'

'With, like, vitamin-fortified cereal and educational television?' I asked, my eyes wide. My voice hardened. 'You didn't offer us a home and a family. You offered us a school, where we could be studied. Next question.'

'It would be patriotic of you to help your country,' the blond woman said stiffly.

'And it would be nice if the Easter Bunny were real,' I answered. 'But it's interesting that you've gone from wanting to study us to wanting us to help our country. Next question.'

The woman flushed, and I saw several colleagues look at her as if she had messed up.

'Frankly, we consider you a national resource,' said a woman in uniform. 'A national treasure, if you will.' She gave an unconvincing smile. 'Like the Declaration of Independence.'

I sighed. 'Which is kept in a sealed display case under lock and key, with armed guards. No, thanks. Anyone else?'

The cool-eyed general spoke again. 'The fact remains that you are minors, and as such must be under adult supervision and guardianship, according to state law. We're offering you such guardianship with a great many benefits and privileges. There could be many less-attractive options.' He sat back looking satisfied, as if he had just crushed an opponent at Battleship.

I blinked and looked around the room in disbelief. 'You're *kidding,*' I said. 'We've escaped from top-security prisons, lived through mental and physical *torture,* lived on our own for *years,* made tons of smarty-pants grown-ups look like fools without even trying, eaten *desert rats* with *no* A1 steak sauce, and you're telling me we're *minors* and have to have *guardians?*' I shook my head, staring at him. 'Listen, pal, I grew up in a freaking *dog crate*. I've seen horrible part-human mutations die gut-wrenching deaths. I've had people, mutants, and robots trying to kill me twenty-four/seven for as long as I can remember, and you think I'm gonna cave to *state law?* Are you *bonkers?*'

My voice had risen steadily and it filled the room. Everyone was stock-still, dead quiet.

Finally the man who had first greeted us cleared his throat uncomfortably. 'Well, perhaps we should take a break and meet again tomorrow.' It was like someone looking at a horrible battlefield wound and saying, 'Let's put a Band-Aid on this thing, patch it right up!'

Once we were back in the limousine, my mom patted my hand and said brightly, 'Gosh, that went well!' and I snorted.

Then we were all laughing, and I wished we could stay that way forever: all together and laughing. Of course, we couldn't.

CHAPTER TEN

That night we decided to order in pizza like normal people.

Mom had a menu from a local place, and each of us kids got to order our own whole, large pizza. I would never get used to having enough to eat for more than a day or two at a time. It wouldn't last, so I was going to enjoy it while I could.

'So, this whole government-control thing isn't working for me,' I said while we waited for the delivery guy to show up.

My mom looked at me. 'I'd feel better if you were being protected somehow,' she said. See? That's what kind of mom she is. She doesn't order me to do stuff, doesn't try to pin me down. As long as I don't leave my socks lying around, I'm golden.

'Their protection never *lasts*,' said Gazzy. 'It turns into something else. Like a trap, or a nightmare, or an experiment. Did I remember to order extra pineapple?'

The rest of the flock nodded.

'I don't want to go to school,' said Nudge, pulling her attention away from a TV show. 'Unless it's, like, fashion school or music school, like how to be a rock star. But math class every day? And spelling? Bleah.'

'I don't think those people really know what they want,' said Angel thoughtfully.

'Did we remember to get garlic bread?' Total asked, and we all nodded again.

'But you're not picking up out-and-out evil?' I asked Angel. Having a six-year-old mind reader does come in handy.

'No,' Angel said, stroking Total's back. 'I can feel secrets, and confusion. But no mad-scientist stuff.'

'Something new and different,' said Iggy.

'Anyone want refills on lemonade?' Jeb asked, holding out the carton.

'I do.' Gazzy handed him a cup, and Iggy said, 'No, the blue one's mine.'

Gazzy pushed him the blue cup, then looked up as we all realized that no one had mentioned cup colors. Iggy picked up his cup and drank, not seeming to notice anything odd.

'Which blue cup, Ig?' I asked casually. 'Light or dark?'

'Light,' he said.

We were all silent, and then Iggy frowned. 'Huh. Did you guys tell me what colors the cups were?'

'Nope,' I said quietly.

He stared at the table, then shook his head. 'I'm still—I still can't see squat. No vision. Nothing.' He reached out his hand, moving it slowly until he felt his cup. 'But this cup is blue.'

Gazzy pushed over another cup. 'What's this one?'

Iggy felt for it, then closed his hand around it. 'Yellow?'

'Yeah,' Fang said. 'How about this?' He put the pizza menu into Iggy's hand. 'What color is it?'

'Green?' Iggy asked. 'It feels green.'

No one said anything for a while as we digested this new development. I remembered what Jeb had said, about how we might be mutating on our own, without planning. Nudge seemed to be thinking the same thing. She timidly reached out her hand, and when it was a few inches away, her fork flew into her grasp.

'Have you guys been playing in toxic waste again?' Fang asked severely, putting his hands on his hips.

Nudge giggled. 'No.'

'Been bitten by a radioactive spider?' Fang went on. 'Struck by lightning? Drink a super-soldier serum?'

'No, no, no,' said Iggy. He started reaching for things around the table, and his hand landed on Total. 'You're black.'

'I prefer canine-American,' said Total. 'When's that pie coming? I'm starving.'

'What about me?' Nudge asked, putting Iggy's hand on her face.

He smiled. 'You're sort of a chocolate-milk-slash-coffee color,' he said in wonder.

'Like, mocha,' said Gazzy.

So there you go. Iggy had a new, unexpected skill, like Nudge. Would we all develop them? Surely nothing *more* could happen to Angel—she was pretty much already loaded for bear in terms of special powers.

The rest of us would have to wait and see.

Then the doorbell rang, and we all leaped up. Dinner!

CHAPTER ELEVEN

The flock stood out of sight of the door while Jeb answered it. A short guy in a red shirt stood there holding a large stack of pizza boxes. Jeb paid him, and the guy handed over the pizzas and hurried back to his car. Mom took the boxes, and Jeb shut and locked the door. The flock came out of hiding as if we were Munchkins and the good witch Glinda had just showed up.

'Yes, yes, yes,' Nudge breathed, almost jumping up and down. The incredible smell of pizza filled the room.

Mom put the boxes on the table and opened one. 'Who got the extra pepperoni and mushrooms?'

'Me, me!' I said, feeling my stomach

rumble.

My mom reached into the box, and Gazzy grabbed her arm and said, 'Wait!'

'Get away from that pizza!' I ordered Gazzy, moving closer. 'Yours is probably next.'

'No,' said Gazzy, a stricken look on his face. 'Look!' He pointed into the pizza box, and when I looked closely, I could see a tiny bit of green wire sticking out from under the thick Sicilian crust.

'Take cover!' I yelled, and then we all dove.

Everything flashed brilliant white, and then a huge *kaboom!* practically punctured my eardrums. I was lying on the floor behind the couch, and Fang was behind me, his arms around me, one hand covering my face. There was a bit of crackling, and then the weird post-explosion silence that sounds much louder than ordinary silence. Slight fluttering sounds told me that bits of stuff were floating to the ground.

'You okay?' Fang said, but my ears were blown and muffled, and it sounded as though he was speaking through a pillow. I nodded and scrambled up.

'Report!' I said, then instantly choked on the fine dust that filled the air. I started coughing hard, tears streaming down my face, and every time I took a breath, I sucked in more dust and coughed more.

'I'm okay,' said Nudge, crawling out from

the hallway where she had dived.

'I'm okay,' said Iggy, though I couldn't see him. Then a pile of dust and debris moved on the floor, and he stood up, looking as if he'd been flocked. Like a Christmas tree.

'Okay here,' said Gazzy, and he started coughing too.

'What was *that?*' my mom asked, sounding shocked.

'Everyone all right?' Jeb asked, brushing stuff off his shoulders.

Amazingly, we were all fine, except for minor scrapes, cuts, and bruises. Total looked as if he'd been breaded in preparation for frying. If Gazzy hadn't seen that wire, we all would have resembled pizzas ourselves: flat and messy.

'But what *was* that?' my mom asked again. She looked totally freaked out and kept patting everyone down for broken bones.

'A welcome wagon?' I said, already gathering our meager belongings. 'Okay, everyone. Let's scram before the cops show.'

CHAPTER TWELVE

We split up from Mom and Jeb, then met them fifteen minutes later at an inconspicuous motel out on the highway. They drove, and we flew overhead, looking for anyone tailing them. We didn't see anyone, and I guessed that whoever set up the bomb assumed it had worked and that we had all been eliminated. No one had tried to blow us up in a while, and we were all a little shaken. It was a reminder that danger could come from anywhere, anyone.

After brushing themselves off as much as possible, Mom rented a room, and Jeb rented the one next door. We waited till the coast was totally clear, and then the flock and Total sneaked in. Maybe we'd be safe here for a little while.

That night, my mom and I stayed up talking after everyone else had gone to bed. I curled up on the couch next to her and tried not to imagine what my life would have been like if I could have been talking to her like this all the time.

'Who could have done that?' she asked, still looking upset and troubled.

I shrugged. 'It could be anyone. Any of the bad guys, any of the good guys who are really bad guys, anyone working for any of them. Maybe the government gang didn't want to take no for an answer.'

She shook her head. 'I still feel that no matter how overbearing they are, how much they don't understand the situation, they're on the level. I don't think they were behind this.'

'Do you trust Jeb?' I asked her.

'I do,' she said slowly. 'But I also think you should always be on guard. With everyone, all the time.'

I nodded. 'I'm not sure what we'll do, after this.'

'The government school still not holding any appeal for you?' She smiled.

'No.'

'You're always welcome at home,' she said, and took my hand.

I shook my head. 'I wouldn't do that to you—at least not too often. Anyone who helps us winds up getting hurt. Like tonight, for example.'

'Still. Never forget you have a refuge.'

'Okay,' I said with a smile. 'I wish we could hang out like this more often.'

'Me too. There's so much I want to talk to you about, so much I don't know.' She hesitated. 'Is there something going on between you and Fang?'

My eyes went wide, and I felt heat flush my cheeks. 'No. What do you mean?' I said unconvincingly.

My mom stroked my hair and tried not to look worried. 'Just be careful,' she said, and kissed my forehead. 'There are other kinds of pain besides physical.'

Oh, like I didn't know that.

CHAPTER THIRTEEN

'Yo, Max.'

Fang. Fang's voice. I blinked and sat up fast, grabbing the sheets. 'Wha'?' I panted. 'What's, what's—'

'Let's take a little spin.' Fang motioned outside. I looked around. The girls were sleeping in this room, boys in the other. Outside, the night was deep but bright with moonlight.

'Why?' I whispered.

He smiled unexpectedly, and my heart gave a little squeeze. 'Because we can.'

Sadly, I usually don't need a better reason than that. Fang eased himself through the motel door and ran off into the night, while I quickly pulled on jeans and a jacket. Then I followed him, raced toward the dark part of the parking lot, and launched myself into the air.

My wings snapped out, full and strong, through the big slits in my jacket. I dipped several feet until my feathers gathered the air like sails, and then I rose powerfully over the rooftops of this quiet DC suburb. I smiled as I cut through the night sky, Fang a thousand feet above me, barely outlined by moonlight. In seconds I had reached him, full of the

43

exhilaration that comes with free flying, flying for pleasure. Instead of for escape, for example.

We wheeled through the chilly air, not speaking, leaving the town far behind.

Soon we were near the ocean, close to Chesapeake Bay. Swooping lower in wide circles, we saw a small unused dock jutting out into the water. With unspoken agreement we coasted lower, finally making a sneaker-pounding running stop down the length of the dock. Scarcely breathing hard, we sat on the edge of the dock, leaving our wings outstretched to cool off. There was no room— one of Fang's wings overlapped one of mine.

'This is pretty.' My feet dangled at least a yard above the water.

'Yeah. Peaceful.' Fang was looking at everything except me. 'Are we back on track?'

I looked at him. 'What do you mean? What track?'

'You and me. We . . . broke up.'

Oh, that. I gazed at the water, embarrassed.

'I don't want to split up again,' he said.

'No, me neither.'

'Max . . .'

His face was unreadable in the moonlight. I felt the light, feathery heat of his wing lying over mine. What did he want from me? Why couldn't he just let things be?

'What do you want from me?' he said.

44

'What do I—What do you mean? I want the usual stuff, like always.' I *hated* conversations like this, *hated* talking about my feelings unless I was, like, furious. Then words came easily. But this mushy hearts-and-flowers stuff? Ugh.

His eyes met mine. 'Look, you didn't like it when you saw me with that girl at school, back in Virginia.'

True. Seeing Fang kissing the Red-Haired Wonder had sent acid churning through my gut. I stayed silent, remembering.

'And I wasn't thrilled about you and Sam, the possible traitor, also back in Virginia.'

'Yeah, Virginia basically sucked,' I agreed.

'Well, why? Why would it bother us to see us with other people?'

Oh, God, where was he going with this? If I had more than brother-sister feelings for Fang, I could barely admit them to myself, much less him.

' 'Cause we're shallow and self-serving?' I tried, wishing he would just drop it.

He rolled his eyes and took my hand. His hand was hard and calloused, tough with muscle and old scars. The night settled around us like a blanket. I could hear the water lapping against the dock. We were totally alone.

'You're . . . ,' he began, and I waited, heart throbbing in my throat. 'Such a *pain,*' he concluded.

45

'*What?*' I asked, just as his head swooped in and his mouth touched mine. I tried to speak, but one of Fang's hands held the back of my head, and he kept his lips pressed against me, kissing me softly but with a Fanglike determination.

Oh, jeez, I thought distractedly. *Jeez, this is Fang, and me, and . . .* Fang tilted his head to kiss me more deeply, and I felt totally lightheaded. Then I remembered to breathe through my nose, and the fog cleared a tiny bit. Somehow we were pressed together, Fang's arms around me now, sliding under my wings, his hands flat against my back.

It was incredible. I loved it. I loved him.

It was a total disaster.

Gasping, I pulled back. 'I, uh—' I began oh so coherently, and then I jumped up, almost knocking him over, and raced down the dock. I took off, flying fast, like a rocket.

CHAPTER FOURTEEN

So there you have it. I was every warning headline of every teen magazine. 'Are you pushing him away? How to get him closer!' 'Tired of being a tomboy? How to access your inner vixen!' 'Not ready for a relationship? Here are 10 ways to tell!' I'm guessing one way to tell would be freaking out over a simple kiss, streaking off in the night, then lying awake in bed until dawn, tortured by emotions you don't even recognize. I don't know—seems like a clue.

When my mom patted my shoulder to 'wake' me up in the morning, my eyes were dry and gritty. I had gotten about twenty minutes of sleep. I was dreading facing Fang, and wondering if he was mad, hurt, or what. Then Mom said, 'Want pancakes? There's an IHOP next door,' and my day started looking up.

It went downhill again after the pancakes. Fang was distant, Iggy kept touching things and yelling out what color they were, and Nudge kept making metal things leap toward her, like the zipper on my hoodie, for example. Gazzy and Angel were being themselves, which, face it, is a challenge even on a good day. Total for once was subdued, curled up on the motel sofa, licking his back.

And yet our Washington DC fun wasn't over! Mom and Jeb convinced us to keep our other meeting, which involved us getting paraded in front of a special congressional committee. I guess it was like the Surprise Mutant Solution Committee.

Anyway.

'We have some exciting news,' a silver-haired man said. 'We've been allocated the funds to create a special school for you. The location hasn't been decided yet. Nor has it been decided whether you will be mainstreamed with other children.' He beamed as if he'd just told us we'd won the lottery.

'Uh-huh,' I said warily.

'I'm still unclear why the children can't just live in peace somewhere, in hiding,' said my mom. *Way to go, Mom!*

'Well, you see, Ms. Martinez—' a woman began.

'Doctor,' said my mom. 'Dr. Martinez.'

'Ah, yes. Dr. Martinez,' the woman said.

'Like in the witness protection program,' my mom went on. 'The government spends millions of dollars, so much time and energy, protecting witnesses who are often criminals themselves. Why can't you make the same effort to protect innocent children?'

Nudge squeezed my hand. All of us had wanted real parents our whole life, and after a couple of disastrous false alarms, I'd actually found mine. And my mom was the best mom in the whole world, ever.

Though even I thought she was going a little far, calling us 'innocent.' Maybe she didn't know about the string of stolen cars or the vandalism of empty vacation homes.

But I digress.

An older woman in a navy suit leaned forward. 'The witness protection program is limited in its scope and not intended to create a suitable environment for children. Which is why we were thinking more of a boarding-school situation, with appropriate guardians and teachers.' She smiled somewhat frostily. 'It will be a most desirable situation, I assure you.'

'We're not convinced that you understand the nature of these children,' said Jeb, speaking up for the first time. 'We're not sure why you believe yourselves to be the best judges of what would be best for them.'

'None of us have been associated, however peripherally, with Itex or its various research branches,' said a dark-haired woman. I thought Jeb flushed a little at that. 'But we've made an extensive study of the situation, of the children, and of various rehabilitation systems that might be applicable here. Many of us are parents ourselves.'

'But you're not *their* parents,' said my mom.

'With all due respect, Dr. Martinez, neither are you, nor is Jeb Batchelder,' said an older man wearing glasses. 'We understand the genetic component, as it's been explained to us. But the fact remains that these children have essentially grown up without any adult who could realistically be called a parental figure.'

Again Jeb flushed, and I wondered how guilty he felt about letting the flock down. I

49

hoped it was *a lot.* I felt my mom tense beside me, and all of a sudden I'd had enough.

Max, I hate this. Can we get out of here?

Angel's voice filtered into my head. I turned to see her big blue eyes pleading with me. Over her head, Fang's eyes met mine, and I gave a barely perceptible nod. As usual, he and I were on the same page without even speaking.

I raised my hand, taking everyone by surprise. You'd think they would have been used to it by now. 'I need to say something.'

CHAPTER FIFTEEN

'You guys are talking about us like we're not even here. You're sitting there deciding our fate without even asking us,' I said.

'Maximum, while children are often encouraged to express a preference, typically, responsible adults determine what's best for them. Children just don't have the life experience or education to understand the big picture.' The silver-haired senator gave me a reassuring smile, which, call me paranoid, I didn't find at all reassuring.

A teen magazine would have encouraged me to get in touch with my inner feelings. So I searched deep within myself and realized that my inner feelings were telling me to punch all of them in the face. Which is why teen magazines just don't seem to apply to my life.

'Life experience?' I repeated tightly. 'Big picture? I've had more life experience in fourteen years than you've had in—what are you, like, a hundred?'

The senator's face started turning pink.

'You're the ones who don't have the life experience,' I said. 'Have you ever woken up with your mouth duct-taped shut, not knowing where you are or where your family is? Are you afraid of everything and everyone? Have you foraged for food in Dumpsters? Do you sleep with one eye open because at any second someone might try to kill you? Have you ever opened a *pizza* box only to find a *bomb?* You guys don't have any *idea.*'

Some of the committee members looked horrified, and I wondered just how complete their files were.

'Angel's only six,' I went on. 'But ten bucks says she's been in more fights to the death than any of you. You guys have unreal ideas about us that you *wish* were true. The kids you designed this school for are probably clean, polite, grateful, agreeable. Sadly, that isn't *us.*'

The flock stood up around me, and I guessed they were all making their toughest faces, the ones that crack me up 'cause they're so cute. But this committee wouldn't know that.

'We don't need to be "rehabilitated,"' I went on. 'We're survivors, and that pretty much cancels out good manners or patience or a burning desire to please. Your fancy school, your plans—none of that has anything to do with us, the real us. You go on and have fun spinning your wheels. But include us *out.*'

I rose and stalked past the line of grown-ups trying to figure out snappy comebacks. *Good luck with that,* I thought. I burst out the heavy door, ready to slug anyone who tried to stop me. But no one did, and I glanced back quickly to see the flock, Total, my mom, and Jeb all hurrying behind me. At the end of the hallway was another conference room. It had huge windows, some of which were cranked open for cleaning or something.

Without thinking, without planning—in other words, in true Max style—I gave my mom a fast, hard hug, put on my jacket, then stepped to the window and jumped out. I thought I heard her gasp, but the sound was torn away by the air rushing past me as I snapped my wings open. Then I was aloft, held securely by the air, supported and cradled by the atmosphere. I couldn't help smiling, pulling cold air into my lungs, feeling free.

'Where are we going, Max?' Gazzy called. My flock was sailing powerfully alongside me, all looking as happy and relieved as I felt.

'Does it matter?' I called back, and he shook his head.

'Didn't think so,' I said to myself, and surged upward.

CHAPTER SIXTEEN

'Look, the Pentagon!' Gazzy said suddenly, pointing. He wheeled into a tight left turn and headed for it. 'I always wanted to see it!'

'Me too!' said Iggy sarcastically, already flying after Gazzy.

'Yeah, you can touch it and feel that it's white,' I said.

The rest of us turned to follow them, and it felt good to see how happy everyone was to be flying.

'Dive-bomb!' Gazzy cried, tucking in his wings and angling downward toward the Pentagon.

'No, Gazzy, don't!' I yelled after him. 'It's a government building! They're even more paranoid than we are!'

Cackling maniacally, Gazzy swooped down to within fifty feet of the Pentagon's roof, then tucked into a fast flip and aimed upward again. The six of us soared and tilted and raced, remembering the tricks we'd learned from the hawks and the bats, performing split-second formations and upside-down turns like the kind swimmers make at the end of the pool.

'Okay,' I called finally. 'Let's head out—'

The air was filled with a roar, and I turned my head to see two jets streaking toward us, their pointy noses looking mean.

'What's wrong with them?' Nudge cried, rushing closer to me.

'We violated the Pentagon's airspace,' Fang guessed as the jets roared closer at incredible speed.

Total, in Fang's arms, nodded. 'I should have stopped you! I, at least, should have known better!'

'Let's get out of here!' I yelled, and we turned as fast as we could, heading away from the Pentagon. I didn't know how determined those jets were, and I didn't know who had scrambled them. Had they been sent automatically to eliminate anything over the Pentagon's airspace? Had the Surprise Mutant Solution Committee not taken no for an answer?

We weren't going to hang around to find out.

'Into the trees!' I called, pointing to where several acres of trees made a weensy forest. By tucking our wings tightly back, we lost altitude like feathery rocks. I spotted several openings among the treetops, and we sank into them, immediately turning sideways and opening our wings so we wouldn't hit the ground. We flew sideways for a while, slipping between tree trunks, knowing we were invisible to the jets.

Unless they had infrared sensors. In which case we were sunk.

'Whee-hah!' Gazzy shouted. It was much harder to fly vertically like this, but we'd all perfected the technique in the past year. Yes, jets can fly sideways too, and faster than we can, I have to admit. But they can't weave in and out of trees, now, can they? Or turn practically on dimes?

No. If they try, they end up exploding in impressive fireballs.

These woods were so small that we had to keep circling and cutting back across them, which we did for about twenty minutes. Finally the noise of the jets lessened, and then it faded altogether. We cautiously left the woods and came to a landing nearby.

'That was awesome!' yelled Gazzy, holding up his hand.

Iggy slapped him a high five (I don't know how he does that—he never misses), and they both cackled in triumph.

'Awesome, and yet stupid,' I said, ever the voice of reason. 'Let's keep under the radar from now on, guys.'

'We *were* under the radar,' Gazzy argued. 'Totally under the radar.'

'I meant metaphorically,' I said. 'Both under

the actual radar and also just low profile, discreet, secret.'

'Uh-huh,' Gazzy said in a tone that told me he hadn't heard a word I had said. 'That was so awesome!'

Reason number 52 why Gazzy isn't the flock leader.

CHAPTER SEVENTEEN

And just like that, we were free again. Or as free as six homeless mutants could be. In three hours we were eight thousand feet over the Pocono Mountains, looking for a place to hang. Once again, a state park saved us. A big patch of green beckoned, and we slipped down through the trees as silently as we could, not far from the park entrance. The sun was setting, and we needed to find a good place to sleep, but there was something I had to do first.

I called my mom to let her know we were okay. Something I'd never, ever had to do before in my life.

'Oh, Max—are you all right?' She had answered her cell phone practically before it rang.

'We're good,' I said. A pang inside me meant that I wished I could be with her but knew I couldn't. I could never be a 'home at five' kind of daughter. 'They were just creeping me out.'

'I know,' my mom said. 'They seem so arrogant. I really don't think they have a good plan for you guys.' She paused, and I guessed she was biting her lip, trying not to ask where we were or where we were headed. Which was good, because as usual, I was operating without a game plan.

'No, me neither,' I said. 'Give Ella a hug for me, okay?'

'Okay, honey,' she said. 'Listen—Jeb is here and he wants to talk to you.'

I made an 'ick' face, and Fang raised his eyebrows at me.

'Max?'

'Yes,' I said reluctantly.

'You're safe?' His voice sounded warm and dad-like.

'Yes.'

'Good.'

'So you're not the Voice in my head?' I asked. 'I saw you be the Voice.'

'I can do the Voice, but I'm not the Voice,' said Jeb. 'That's all part of the larger picture.'

Great. Another puzzle. Good thing I got my kicks out of not understanding *my entire life*.

'Whatever,' I said, knowing that made him crazy.

'Listen, Max,' Jeb said. 'Dr. Martinez—your

57

mom—and I want you to know that we trust you. Your instincts have served you well so far, and kept you and the flock alive. We feel that you'll do the right thing, whether you know you are or not.'

Hmm. Compliments always made me suspicious.

'Oh, yeah?' I said.

'Yes,' he said firmly. 'You're the right person to lead the flock. It's what you were created to do. You're doing a terrific job at it, finding your own way. We trust you to do the right thing now.'

If I could have believed him, it would have warmed the cockles of my little heart. All I had to do was decide to believe him, take him at face value. After all, my mom was right there, hearing him, and I *did* trust her.

'Huh,' I said.

There was a pause, as if he'd been hoping for more.

'Anyway, take care, Max,' he said finally. 'Call your mom or me when you get a chance. We'll be working on things from this end.'

'Working on what?' I asked.

'Oops, we better go,' Jeb said. 'Don't want to stay on the phone too long, in case someone's tracing it. Give my love to the flock.'

The phone clicked and went dead.

I looked up. Fang was watching me. We still

hadn't talked about the Incident of the previous night. Nudge was shifting from one foot to another, the way she did when she got hungry. Total was taking a potty break in the bushes. Everyone looked tired, and we still needed to rustle up food.

Jeb had said that he and my mom trusted me and thought I was doing a good job. He'd said to trust my instincts.

My instincts asked me if he was playing another angle.

CHAPTER EIGHTEEN

After a lame dinner of scavenged food, we settled onto various branches of the tallest trees we could find. Did we sleep in trees a lot? Yes. Had we ever fallen out of a tree while asleep? As amusing as that would have been, no.

I was exhausted, still pretty hungry, and clueless about what the next day would bring. But I double-checked my flock before I let myself relax. Angel and Total were snuggled in the deep vee of an enormous oak. Iggy and Gazzy were close together in the same tree. Nudge was stretched out along a thick branch, one arm hanging down. Fang was—

I looked. He'd been right there a second

59

ago. Now, no Fang.

'Where's Fang?' I tried to keep alarm out of my voice—don't panic till you need to—but I'm so not into the whole missing-flock thing.

Angel and Gazzy looked around, and Fang said, 'I'm right here,' sounding surprised. And there he was, straddling a branch with his back against the trunk.

I blinked. 'I looked—you weren't there.'

'Yes, I was,' he said, eyebrows raised.

'No,' said Nudge. 'I looked for you too. Were you behind the tree?'

'I was right here!' Fang insisted, waving his arms.

'I didn't see you either, man,' Iggy said with a straight face.

I rolled my eyes at him, then said, 'I'm rolling my eyes, Iggy.'

'Well, I was here the whole time,' said Fang, shrugging.

Five minutes later, he disappeared again.

'Fang!' I said, peering all around. True, it was dark, but thanks to raptor vision, we can all see perfectly well at night. Every other flock member was there, clear as day.

'I'm *here*,' said Fang.

There was nothing where his voice was coming from.

'Behind the tree?' I was starting to get irritated.

'Are you blind?' Fang demanded. 'I'm *right*

here!'

And there he was. Complete with a brand-new skill. Let's hear it for spontaneous mutation, folks!

CHAPTER NINETEEN

No, Fang could not actually make himself invisible. It was more like his natural stillness and darkness just sort of made him fade into the background till he kind of disappeared. As soon as he moved again, he was visible. If he stayed still, we could search for an hour, but our eyes would skate right over him.

'I want to do it too!' said Gazzy, sitting very, very quietly, completely motionless.

'Nope,' said Nudge, shaking her head. 'You stand out like a fart in church.'

'Appropriately enough,' I muttered.

'What about me?' Iggy asked. He folded his wings in and went statue still.

'No, you're visible,' I told him.

'Am not!' Iggy said.

I hurled a big prickly pinecone at him and heard it thunk hard against his chest. He howled in pain.

'Could I do that if I couldn't see you?' I pointed out.

'Seriously, you can't see me?' Fang sounded

pleased.

'Not when you're still and quiet,' I admitted.

He smiled big, and it was horrible, seeing only a mouthful of white teeth against the rough tree bark. He shook his head, and bam, there he was, all of him. I started to get an idea of how incredibly annoying he could make himself with this skill.

'Oh, guys, I had a couple thoughts I wanted to go over with you,' I said, suddenly remembering. I heard Total mutter something, but I paid no attention.

Iggy pretended to snore loudly. I threw another pinecone at him.

'Quit throwing things at me!' He rubbed his arm.

'Glad you could join us,' I said. 'Now, listen up. We're on the road again. Erasers don't seem to exist anymore, and we haven't seen any Flyboys. But you know whatever's left of Itex is regrouping and gearing up for the next war. Plus, someone tried to explode us. So, a couple guidelines: We need to move every other day, keep on the go. No staying in one place more than forty-eight hours.'

'Ugh,' Total said. He was curled up in Angel's lap.

'We will not make friends with humans until after the apocalypse,' I went on, ticking items off on my fingers.

'What's the apocalypse?' Gazzy asked.

'Basically, the complete destruction of the world as we know it. And we will not trust humans, even after the apocalypse.'

But Max, you're mostly human, said the Voice.

So were Erasers, I shot back. *Besides, you know what I mean.*

'However,' I went on, 'I do want us to try to recognize the good in things. Like my mom. And Ella. And chocolate-chip cookies. It just seems like we shouldn't let our enemies make us all bitter and full of hate and stuff.'

I waited for everyone to give me a hard time about being all Hallmarky.

'Oh, yeah, ix-nay on the ate-hay,' said Fang.

'Who are you, and what have you done with the real Max?' Iggy asked.

'Ha ha. So I think we should take turns naming three good things that have happened to us. Who wants to start?' I said brightly.

Silence.

'Nudge?'

'Um,' she said.

'Well, dinner was *delicious*,' said Total. I gave him a Look. 'Okay, okay,' he said. 'Um, well, no one tried to kill us today.'

'That's one,' I agreed.

'We're all together,' he said.

'Okay, two. You're doing good. Go on.'

'I don't have fleas.'

I was taken aback. 'Uh, yep, I guess that's

true. That's a good thing.' Couldn't deny it.

Total looked pleased.

'*I* don't have fleas,' said Iggy.

'Bet you do,' Gazzy said.

I sighed as the discussion dissolved into accusations and defenses. I would try again tomorrow. Sometimes this leader stuff was a huge pain in the butt.

CHAPTER TWENTY

Subterranean

The salt dome located a quarter of a mile below the earth's surface could easily have held several football stadiums. Though salt domes occurred naturally in many different places on the globe, this one happened to be beneath a certain country in middle Europe. During World Wars I and II, many national treasures had been stored here to avoid destruction by Allied bombs. Nowadays there was talk of turning this enormous network of caves and tunnels, most as wide as four-lane highways, into an impermeable storage center for radioactive waste.

'Since those fools keep producing nuclear power without having the slightest idea of what to do with its toxic by-products,' the

Uber-Director muttered to himself. His small motorized chair wheeled silently over the smooth crystalline floors. Eventually, perhaps, this cavern would be sold, and the Uber-Director would have to relocate his base of operations. But for right now, this was a most acceptable, and unusually safe, headquarters.

Heavy lines of cable, some almost a foot in diameter, snaked down from the surface, bringing electricity, water, fresh air. In addition, mobile, self-contained air scrubbers hummed quietly as they scooted from room to room, trapping carbon dioxide and releasing oxygen. When they touched a barrier, they simply reversed and scooted off in another direction. The Uber-Director himself didn't use that much oxygen—only 23 percent of his being required oxygen to function. But stale air was unpleasant.

The Uber-Director's conference room was off the main tunnel. It adjoined his actual 'office' and held an antique table whose top had been hewn from a single slab of rosewood. A bank of plasma screens, five wide and four high, covered most of one wall.

'Sir?'

A human assistant stood nearby, head lowered in respect.

'Have the arrangements been made?' asked the Uber-Director.

'Yes, sir. Everything is prepared. The

auction preview can begin at your signal.'

'Excellent. Have all the parties accepted the invitation to attend?'

The assistant straightened proudly. 'Yes, sir. All of them.'

'Then let's begin.'

CHAPTER TWENTY-ONE

Subterranean

Electronic relays responded to the Uber-Director's eye signals. The plasma screens popped on, each framing the leader of a different country or corporation. The men and women on the screens, aware that they were now live on camera, shifted in their seats and adjusted the minuscule microphones in front of them. If any of them were shocked by the Uber-Director's unconventional, even grotesque, appearance, they showed no sign. They had been advised beforehand.

'Greetings,' said the Uber-Director in his odd, machinelike voice.

He interrupted the chorus of responses from his onscreen clients.

'To clarify what we're doing here today, let me go over some salient points.' He turned his chair slightly and looked at another large screen to his right. It came on, showing a picture of six scruffy, scowling children. 'These are the items up for auction. They come as a set. Though the set could be split up, it would not be wise, and would no doubt hamper the success of your mission.'

'Could you detail exactly what we're looking at?' a dictator who had recently made CNN's 'Ten Worst Abusers of Human Rights' list broke in forcefully. 'There have been rumors.'

'You are looking at six juvenile avian-human experiments in recombinant-DNA science. They are the most viable of any that have been produced. They can actually fly like birds.' The Uber-Director blinked twice, and the screen behind him showed a short video of six flying children. He was gratified by the gasps and murmurs coming from the viewers, but his 'face' showed no expression. 'They fly well,' he went on. 'They have an uncanny sense of direction and superior regenerative and healing powers. They're smart, wily, and relatively sturdy.'

'You sound as if you admire them.' A woman who had been nicknamed 'the Iron Maiden of Silicon Valley' leaned forward.

'Admire?' said the Uber-Director. 'No. Not at all. To me they are genetic accidents, mistakes.' No one dared mention his own form. 'Nor am I so foolish as to underestimate them, as my predecessors have.'

There were a few seconds of silence, as the potential bidders contemplated the Uber-Director and the possibilities of his offered product. Then he blinked again, and the screen behind him went blank.

'You have received your packets of information,' he said. 'I will answer no more questions. I will alert you as to when and where the bidding will take place. Please be aware that the *opening* bid is five hundred million dollars.'

More murmurs broke out from the wall of screens.

The Uber-Director permitted himself a slight smile. 'After all, it is difficult to put a price on the ability to rule the world.'

CHAPTER TWENTY-TWO

Terranean

'The demonstration is ready, sir.' The assistant stood with head typically bowed, barely managing to avoid saying 'My Lord' or even 'Your Grace.' That was the trouble with old-fashioned humans. Too ruled by emotion, too easily cowed. There would be no place for them in the New Age.

With a blink, the Uber-Director gave

permission to begin.

Ten yards above him, a slight shadow signaled an existing cave. His informants had told him the bird kids often rested in caves. He hoped this demonstration would be more successful than the last.

'Why hasn't it beg—' he started to ask, only to have a movement catch his eye and draw it upward. He looked directly at the rock wall but saw nothing. Then—there! The camouflage was excellent. Only a small patch of skin matrix was visible as the soldier moved sideways across the rock, like a crab. By focusing intently and increasing his internal zoom by 400 percent, the Uber-Director could now see a swarm of soldiers moving toward the opening in the rock face.

One of them had shot a fine, almost invisible net over the cave opening. The Uber-Director smiled. Even at this magnification, he had to concentrate hard to see the occasional patches of matrix. His assistant frowned and squinted at the rock wall. An ordinary human would have a great deal of trouble spotting these new soldiers.

With his mind, the Uber-Director turned on a channel that allowed him to listen in on the coded transmissions between the soldier units. This generation, Generation J, had been endowed with some intelligence and only rudimentary emotion, but they seemed to be using and channeling them more effectively than their predecessors.

They were much more controllable than either Erasers or their flying-machine replacements, and smart enough to make quick decisions and improvise.

Earlier versions had been smarter—too smart. Smart enough to question orders, to want to make their own decisions. Others had had only a machine's ability to follow orders. Their ability to think on their feet, to make snap decisions, to adapt to changing circumstances, had been practically nonexistent.

Even more disastrous had been Generations D through G. Either they were so blood hungry that they couldn't be controlled once they scented their prey, or their empathy was so heightened that they couldn't bring themselves to actually kill anything.

The soldiers paused, patched into one impulse, one global command. Then they quickly detached the netting and sprang into the cave entrance. Moving as one, they left no space to escape.

Several of the units reappeared at the cave's entrance. They tossed down mannequins filled with hamburger, buzzing with flies. They had not eaten them. They had followed their orders and captured their prey. Now they raised their arms in victory.

The Uber-Director blinked at his assistant,

70

who was gazing at the mannequins with dismay and revulsion.

'Yes, sir.' The assistant opened a small black suitcase. It contained a highly efficient electric generator.

The Uber-Director sent his soldiers the message, and instantly they swarmed down the rock wall like spiders, moving surely and easily over a surface with few ridges, no handholds.

The assistant was afraid of them but knew not to show it. The soldiers circled him, their faces expressionless.

'Here,' the assistant muttered nervously. One soldier stepped forward, his left shoulder turned to the assistant. Hands trembling slightly, the assistant hooked the generator to the soldier's shoulder and turned it on. A quick burst of electricity made the soldier jolt and stiffen, then relax. His face smoothed. The next soldier stepped up.

A burst of electricity acted like a drug on this series, both exciting and calming them. The soldiers craved it, and it was a useful reward. When they didn't get it, their behavior became unpredictable and violent. It was a drawback, a design flaw.

But one they were working on.

CHAPTER TWENTY-THREE

'Where are we headed next, Max?' Nudge carefully turned her hot dog over the small open fire.

I had been thinking about just that all day. 'Chili?' I stirred the open can, nestled among the burning embers, with a clean, peeled stick.

Gazzy held out his hot dog and I glopped some chili onto it. Not a tidy process.

'Let's go back to France,' said Nudge. 'I loved France.'

'Yeah, France was nice,' I agreed. 'Except for the four Itex branches.'

Recently we'd done the Bird Kids' Whirlwind Tour of Europe, focusing on various spots for imprisonment and abuse, run by madmen and madwomen under the guise of the Itexicon Corporation, mingled with pastry and trendy European fashion. Our lives were nothing if not eclectic.

'How about Canada?' Iggy suggested. 'Seems cool.'

'Hm,' I said. To tell the truth, I hadn't actually decided yet. Nowhere seemed far enough away from Itex minions or the School or the Institute or any of the other faceless entities that seemed bent on using or destroying us. I wanted to get far, far away from everyone.

Iggy felt for trash on the ground, stuffing it into a plastic grocery bag. I heard him mutter, 'White. Tan. Ooh, clear, weird. Tan. Blue,' as he touched various things.

'Oh, guess what,' said Angel, taking a bite of hot dog. Hearing those words from Angel always made me tense up. 'I have a new skill!'

Oh, great. Fang and I made appalled faces at each other over Angel's head.

'You mean—besides the talking-to-fish stuff?' I asked cautiously.

She nodded.

Oh, holy mud, I thought, hoping she hadn't suddenly developed the ability to shoot lightning out of her eyes. Or something.

'Um, what is it?' *Please let me not freak out at the answer.*

'Look.' She raised her head and looked up into my face. The whole flock leaned closer, watching her. I searched Angel's face, praying that horns wouldn't pop out of her forehead. I was about to ask what her skill was, when I saw it.

'See?' she said.

'Uh, yeah,' I answered, staring. Staring at her smooth, tan skin, dark brown eyes, her much straighter brown hair.

'I can change how I look!' she said unnecessarily.

'Uh-huh, yep, I see that,' I said.

73

'Show them bird girl,' said Total. 'I love that one.'

Angel smiled. While we all waited, holding our breath, she began to change again. Two minutes later, we had a blue bird of paradise with Angel's eyes. I mean, she still had a human shape. But her face and head were covered with fine turquoise feathers and she had two spectacular plumes. It was the weirdest freaking thing I'd ever seen, and believe me when I tell you, that's saying something.

She held out slender feathery hands and wiggled her fingers.

'Oh, my God,' breathed Nudge. 'That is so awesome.'

Angel smiled and, just as quickly, turned back into herself. 'So far I can only do those two,' she said. 'But I bet if I practice, I can do other stuff.'

'Uh-huh,' I said weakly.

'How come she can do that and I can't?' the Gasman asked.

'You're siblings, not twins,' I said, giving mental thanks.

'We're all changing a lot,' said Nudge, sounding worried. 'We're changing in ways they didn't plan, didn't expect.'

'Yeah,' said Iggy. 'By the end of the week, we'll be tadpoles.'

'Iggy,' said Nudge, 'I'm serious. We don't

know what's going to happen to us.'

I looked at my flock. Fang was guarded; the rest looked varying degrees of anxious. Time to put on my leader hat.

'Listen up, guys,' I said, sounding calm and in charge. I should be on Broadway, I really should. 'It's true we're changing, and in ways they didn't program. And we have no idea what's going to happen next. But you know what? No one else does either. It's the *one* way that we're like the rest of all the people out there.' I waved my arms to demonstrate 'world.'

'No one *ever* knows what's going to happen next,' I went on. 'People change all the time, and they're not sure how they'll end up. They might be short or tall, able to play the piano or not; they might have their mom's eyes or their dad's nose or their uncle's bald spot. It's *always* a mystery. It's the one constant, everywhere, with everyone. We're just a little more exciting, a little cooler than most.'

Was I good or was I good?

My flock looked calmer, more cheerful. They nodded and smiled.

'Okay, now,' I said more briskly. 'Time for bed.' I held my fist out. One by one, my flock stacked theirs on top, and then we headed up into the trees to sleep the sleep of the innocent.

Well, okay, maybe not so innocent. But the

sleep of the much less guilty than others, for sure.

CHAPTER TWENTY-FOUR

You are reading Fang's Blog. Welcome!
You are visitor number: 98,345

Greetings, faithful readers. This site has had over 600,000 hits, which is unbelievable. It's not like we're here dropping Mentos into Coke bottles or anything. This is just us. But I'm glad you've tuned in.

The big news of today is that we've all decided to settle down and go to regular school and stuff, and Fox is going to make a reality TV series out of it, called *Bird Kids in the House!* They'll have like a hundred cameras all over the place, and they can film Iggy cooking and Angel doing her weird stuff, and Total listening to his iPod.

They can film Max leading.

Nah, I'm just kidding. No reality series. Our lives are probably a little *too* real for most people, if you know what I'm saying. Although, hey, if anyone from Fox is reading this, make us an offer!

We're not sure what's going to happen next. After our weird meetings in DC, we're craving more fresh air and fewer desk jockeys. But it's starting to occur to me (forgive me if I've been a little slow) that maybe we, the flock, I mean, should be working toward something besides just trying to eat enough every day. For a long time, our goal was to find our parents. And look how well *that* turned out for us. Now we're fresh out of goals, and you know what? It feels a little—tame. I mean, if we're not out there butting heads with the buttheads that are destroying the world, then what are we doing? What's our point? Why are we here?

Granted, our options are somewhat limited, given the number of people who want to kill us, or worse. Plus, I understand there are pesky child-labor laws that will get in our way. Frankly, though we can do all sorts of cool stuff, we're not actually qualified for a lot of occupations. Like, any occupation that requires actual education. Which pretty much leaves the entertainment industry.

But I've been thinking . . . maybe we could become spokesmutants. For different causes. We could be the poster children for both animal *and* child abuse, for example.

If anyone has any answers, drop me a line.
—Fang out

Part Two

ICE PRINCES AND PRINCESSES

CHAPTER TWENTY-FIVE

Max. Fly to these coordinates. I rubbed my eyes, hoping it had been a dream. Then a topographic map flashed into my brain, even as the Voice gave the directions. I groaned inwardly, hoping the Voice could hear it. So much for our bit of downtime. As I watched the flock slowly wake up, the Voice continued to give me instructions.

Then it said something amazing. *Your mom is waiting for you.*

'Okay, everyone up!' I said, clapping my hands. 'Up and at 'em! It's a whole new day!'

'I'm hungry,' said Nudge, yawning. 'You know what would be good? Like, one of those sausage McHeart-Attack things. The biscuit things. I want about eight of 'em.' She stood up and balanced on her branch, brushing off jeans that had long since reached the 'grimy' crisis point.

'We'll eat on the way,' I said. 'The Voice says we have to go someplace, meet my mom.'

'Could it be a trap?' Angel looked worried.

'It can *always* be a trap, sweetie,' I said, and jumped out into the air.

Trap, schmap. The glory of flying was still the glory of flying. This morning was crisp, cold, and drenched with sunlight. We flew above the clouds for almost an hour, making one fueling stop at a fast-food place. (If I were a bazillionaire, I'd start a chain of healthy fast-food restaurants, except stuff on the menu would actually taste good and people would want to eat it. Smoothies, little dumplings. I could go on.)

But this morning was so beautiful that we couldn't worry about whether we were flying toward a trap or whether our clothes needed washing. This morning it was us plus air, and we soared and floated and played in updrafts, and it was as though all the jagged puzzle pieces of our weird lives had come together perfectly, here and now.

You're off course. Correct by three degrees, south-southwest.

I shifted my left wing slightly and adjusted our course, and the others followed me. An hour later, we were at our coordinates. Which corresponded to a private landing strip carved into the middle of thick woods, not far from Pittsburgh. A small, gleaming white jet sat on the lone runway. Two men in orange jumpsuits were moving traffic cones, yellow flags tucked under their arms. It all seemed oh so familiar, if you know what I'm saying. I mean, how many secret landing strips are tucked into hiding places all across America? Why isn't someone keeping track of this stuff?

I paused in midair, my eyes narrowing.

Then I saw my mom come out of the plane, looking up at the sky, shading her eyes.

'Doesn't look very trappy,' said Nudge.

'No—but be on guard, just in case,' Fang said.

I nodded and angled my wings back along my body, losing altitude fast. I didn't know what was waiting for us, but I was ready to find out.

CHAPTER TWENTY-SIX

'Max!'

I hoped I would never take my mom's hugs for granted.

'What's going on?' I asked her. 'I thought I wouldn't see you for a while.'

'Me too,' she said. 'But Jeb and I have come up with an unusual possibility for you guys, and we wanted to see if you were interested.'

'Unusual how?' asked Fang.

'Well, sort of a science trip,' said my mom. 'A science trip where you would work with scientists in a pretty remote place. We think it would be kind of fun for you guys, plus you would be useful to the scientists, plus this place is so remote that we think you'd be safer than usual while you're there.'

'Huh.' This was an interesting idea. I'd been

wondering what our next step would be, and here it was, being offered to me. My mom was actually recommending it to me, and unless she'd recently been replaced by an evil clone (possible but unlikely), that meant it was probably a good idea.

'Where's this remote place?' Fang asked.

Mom grinned. 'I'd like to keep that a secret until you're almost there. To help you keep an open mind. And now I'd like you to meet one of the scientists.' She turned to gesture to a woman waiting by the plane's entrance ramp.

The woman was a couple inches shorter than me, with blond hair in a single braid down her back. Though her face was unsmiling, her eyes roamed over us hungrily: the bird kids, the mutant freaks, something she'd never seen before. She blinked when Iggy put Total down on the ground, and I got the feeling she really hadn't known what to expect from us.

But then, most people don't.

'I'm Dr. Brigid Dwyer,' she said, stepping forward and holding out her hand. She seemed awfully young to be a doctor.

'I'm Max.' I shook her hand, and I swear, she looked at mine like it was cotton candy. Then she realized it was just a hand, and the excitement faded a little from her eyes. 'What's this science field trip about?'

She nodded to the jet. 'I'll explain once we're on board.'

Uh-huh. 'How about you explain *before* we get on board?' I asked pleasantly. Yes, Mom had recommended it, but that didn't mean I had gone brain-dead.

Since this was her first Max encounter, I gave Dr. Dwyer a couple moments to find her sea legs.

'Or we could all split now,' I clarified.

'Dr. Martinez'—she gestured to my mother—'has recommended you for a . . . rescue mission.'

'Do tell.' I crossed my arms over my chest, knowing that the flock was scanning the area intently for any signs of danger. 'What—or who—are we rescuing?'

'The world?'

CHAPTER TWENTY-SEVEN

I don't know how many of you have been on private jets, but golly, they're sweet.

'It's a *baby* plane,' Angel whispered when we first got inside the dollhouse-like interior. 'It's going to grow up to be a seven forty-seven someday.'

It was small but very lush, all decked out, similar to the other private jet we'd been on recently. Big flat-screen TV, cushy sofas and armchairs, thick carpeting beneath our feet, little curtains on the little windows. Much nicer than most places we'd stayed in.

Mom had stayed on the ground, and it had been hard—again—to say good-bye to her.

Fang returned from checking out the galley and nodded to me: all clear back there. Gazzy and Iggy had gone forward to the cockpit, and they held the door open to show me a startled pilot, copilot, and navigator. None of whom gave off instant 'I am evil' vibes. Total trotted around sniffing everything, and call me crazy, but that actually made me feel safer.

It's okay, Max, said my Voice. *This is part of the bigger picture. You're being used, but for good this time.*

Oh, that makes it all worthwhile, I thought sarcastically. *Being used for good is so much better than being used for evil. The operative words are still 'being used.'*

The Voice was silent.

'Please, sit down and be comfortable,' said Dr. Dwyer. Like we could avoid it. 'Fasten your seat belts, just for takeoff. As soon as we're in the air, you can have refreshments.'

The flock and I buckled ourselves in, as did Dr. Dwyer.

'Whose plane is this?' I asked.

Dr. Dwyer looked up. 'It belongs to Nino Pierpont,' she said, and my eyebrows went up. Everyone knew he was the world's richest man, richer than any country, company, or

86

family anywhere. So we were either in good hands or totally screwed. Only time would tell. I hoped Mom knew what she was getting us into.

Total jumped up onto the sofa, and Angel buckled his seat belt. Dr. Dwyer watched silently, and I saw her eyes roving over Angel's bulky jacket as if she were wishing a wing would suddenly pop out.

'So where are we going?' I asked. 'Please tell me someplace warm. I've had enough cold weather this winter to last me a lifetime.'

'South America,' said Dr. Dwyer, her eyes not meeting mine. 'Argentina.'

'Rain forest?' I guessed. Argentina was warm, right? This was one of those times when a little schooling would not have been amiss. They turned up every now and then.

'No,' she said. 'We'll be taking a boat from there.'

'A boat?' Fang asked. 'To where?'

'How about something to eat?' Dr. Dwyer undid her seat belt and stood up.

Fang and I looked at each other, then nodded.

We agreed: *Be on guard.*

87

CHAPTER TWENTY-EIGHT

'Are we there yet?' Total grumbled as I held him in my arms.

It was nighttime in Argentina. Cooping up six bird kids in a weensy plane for hours had been a mistake on Dr. Dwyer's part. We'd gotten twitchier and twitchier as the long flight went on, and when we finally touched down in San Julián, Gazzy had burst through the emergency exit, setting off alarms and making the inflatable ramp deploy.

We had then resisted her efforts to get us into a car. Yeah, yeah, we'd signed up to save the world, but that didn't mean we had to agree to being in a small enclosed space again.

Which was why we were flying low over Dr. Dwyer's Jeep, trying to stay out of sight of the scarce traffic on this winding, narrow road. It was dark, cold, and windy. Maybe parts of Argentina, like up north, were warm, but down here close to the tip, it was cold. Great.

In just a few minutes, we were at the ocean, the same ocean that we'd swum in off the East Coast of America. But this was the South Atlantic Ocean, and that had been the North. This part of the ocean had chunks of real ice floating in it. I gritted my teeth, beginning to get why my mom had kept our destination a secret.

Dr. Dwyer drove her Jeep onto a broad dock. A large boat was tethered at the end of it, or maybe it was a small ship. Who knows? The Jeep stopped, and Dr. Dwyer got out, peering up at the sky, looking for us. We circled high above the area, searching for signs of danger, but everything was quiet. Finally we came to gentle landings about thirty feet from her. Total immediately jumped down and began sniffing the dock.

'You really can fly,' Dr. Dwyer said softly, almost to herself.

I shook out my wings, feeling the heat from exercise course through them.

'Well, it's not just an elaborate hoax,' I said.

'It's . . . very beautiful,' she said, then seemed surprised at herself for saying it. Smiling slightly, she shook her head and began to walk with us toward the boat. 'I'm sorry. I know being able to fly wasn't your choice, and I know only some of the trauma you've endured because of it. But to me, on the outside, it seems both beautiful and enviable.'

No one had ever put it that way before, and I didn't know what to say. She sorta seemed to get the whole pluses/minuses thing of being a bird kid. Not many people did.

'This is our research vessel,' said Dr. Dwyer, pointing at the waiting boat. 'We're from the International Earth Science Foundation.'

Frankly, 'research vessel' seemed like a twenty-five-cent name for a ten-cent boat. It was big, maybe a hundred and fifty feet long, but it looked old and run-down. Huge rust stains streaked its blue sides, even covering part of its name: the *Wendy K.* It had a crane-type thingy on the back, and a built-up cabin up front with lots of satellite antennas on top. Where was Nino Pierpont when you needed him to finance a cutting-edge research vessel, for crying out loud?

'We bought her as a retired offshore fishing trawler,' Dr. Dwyer explained as a man came out onto the deck and waved down at us. 'Hey, Michael.'

'Yo, Brigid!' he called back with a smile. His eyes raked us curiously, and I could almost feel his excitement.

'But we've retrofitted her, mostly through donations, and now she's one of our best research stations.' Dr. Dwyer went to the edge of the dock and grabbed a small metal ladder attached to the side of the *Wendy K.* She began to climb up it, and I was sure her hands would be covered with rust when she got to the top. 'It's safe, I assure you,' she told us over her shoulder.

'Maybe. Maybe not,' Gazzy muttered. He flexed his wings, gave a little jump, and flew up to the deck, some eighteen feet above us.

Dr. Dwyer and Michael stared at him, then

exchanged pleased smiles, as if they'd just discovered some neat new life-form.

Total jumped into my arms, and the rest of us flew up also.

'Oh, my God,' Michael said. 'It's true!'

'Well, it's not just an elaborate hoax,' said Dr. Dwyer. 'Michael, this is Max, Fang, Iggy, the, uh, Gasman, Nudge, and Angel. Guys, this is Dr. Michael Papa, one of our leading research scientists.'

Total growled softly.

'Oh, and this is their dog, Total,' she added.

Total sucked in his breath with disgust.

'Thank you for coming,' Dr. Papa said simply. He shook hands with us all, very formally, but he seemed warm and friendly, and not like he might want to stick us in cages and poke us with needles. For example.

'We still don't know why we're here,' I told him.

'Brigid didn't tell you?' Dr. Papa's eyebrows rose. 'You're here to help us gather data for a research project—about global warming and its effects on Antarctica, among other places.' He grinned at us, his teeth pale but human sized in the moonlight. 'You're here to help us save the world.'

CHAPTER TWENTY-NINE

'This is just like *Moby Dick*!' Nudge exclaimed happily, bouncing on her tiny bunk. 'They were on a fishing boat, and we're on a fishing boat too! Only this one doesn't have sails. And isn't made of wood. And we have radar and computers and stuff. Still. We have little bunks, like old-fashioned sailors, and we eat in the mess, and the bathroom is called the head, and it's all boat stuff, everywhere!'

'Dr. Dwyer and Dr. Papa seem nice,' said Angel. She peered through the small porthole above her bed. If we punched out the glass, we could probably escape through it. Just a thought. 'They're really sincere and mean everything they say.'

The rumbling of the ship's engines made the floor vibrate beneath our feet.

'We're headed for the South Pole!' Gazzy jumped over the low threshold into our room from the boys' room next door. 'And it's, like, so far south that it's the bottom of the whole world.'

I tried to keep from groaning out loud. I really, really hate cold weather. I hate bundling up. I'm more of a beach-and-sun kind of girl.

'But you know, if the world is round,' said

Nudge, 'then there's no real top or bottom to it. The South Pole could just as easily be at the top of the world. We could be thinking of everything completely upside down.'

'You're making my head hurt,' Total complained.

Fang and Iggy came in. Iggy was running his fingers gently along every surface, memorizing his surroundings, how many steps to here and there, where furniture was.

'It's small in here,' he complained. 'I feel like we're inside a submarine. Can't we sleep in hammocks on the deck?'

'It's really cold out there,' I reminded him, trying not to sound too bitter.

'Frankly, I'd rather be in Hawaii,' Total griped, and I silently agreed with him. 'Can your Voice send us *there?* We could be lying on a beach on Kauai, with drinks with little umbrellas in them. Instead we're literally at the *end of the world,* doing God knows what. And what's the food gonna be like on this boat?' He shook his head. 'I am not into this plan, I can tell you—'

Suddenly he stopped, and his eyes widened. 'Well, alo-*ha*,' he breathed.

Dr. Papa—that name still cracked me up—was standing in our doorway. At his side, a snow-white Malamute was sizing us up with the practiced eye of a guard dog. Total stared at it, speechless.

'I know it's not the Hilton, but it's not too bad,' Dr. Papa said with a smile. 'We'll try to make you as comfortable as possible. Now, if you've settled in, we can gather in the conference room. You can meet everyone, and we can try to answer your questions.' Dr. Papa scratched the Malamute behind its small triangular ears. 'This is Akila, our mascot and official rescue dog.'

'Does she talk?' Angel asked. A perfectly reasonable question.

Dr. Papa looked startled. 'Uh, no.' He gave Angel an uncertain glance. Total was still dumbstruck, his mouth hanging open. 'Come join us, okay? Go up to the deck, and the conference room is in the forward cabin hatch.' He left, and Akila trotted after him.

'Akila's pretty,' Angel said. 'Like a white teddy bear.'

'Pretty? She's a goddess!' Total said hoarsely.

'You're drooling on Angel's bed,' said the Gasman.

Total swallowed. 'Oh, my God, she's magnificent. Did you see her cheekbones? That fur, brighter than sunlight . . .'

Iggy rolled his eyes.

'Um, Total?' I tried. 'Akila's really pretty and all, but you know, she's just a regular dog, and . . .'

Total jerked upright, his eyes blazing.

'*Regular dog!* She's *perfection!* Don't you ever call her 'regular' again! Is the Venus de Milo just a statue? Is the *Mona Lisa* just a painting? Is the Louvre just a museum?'

'No, it was neat,' Nudge agreed.

I sighed, deciding to drop this hot potato for the time being. 'Okay, everyone, let's go find out what they want us to do. With any luck, we can quickly save the world and still have time to make the hot-air balloon festival in New Mexico. I've always wanted to see that.' Plus, it was *warm* there.

'Cool,' Fang agreed, and we headed off to discover our mission.

CHAPTER THIRTY

The *Wendy K.* was not the Love Boat. It had no casino, no swimming pool, no shopping atrium. It had a small gray-painted kitchen/dining hall, a small gray-painted lounge with a couple of ratty built-in couches, and a small white-painted conference room with some chipped Formica tables, a whiteboard, and some bookcases with bars across the front so the books wouldn't fly off the shelves in rough seas.

'Welcome,' Dr. Dwyer said, indicating some seats. There were seven adults in the room.

Akila was lying on the floor beneath Dr. Papa's chair. Total had paused before we entered, puffed out his chest, then sauntered in as if he were a Russian wolfhound. Since he's a small black Scottie, it was an odd effect.

All the grown-ups were staring at us, which we were used to.

'Please, sit down,' said Michael. 'As you know, I'm Dr. Michael Papa, but you can call me Michael. You know Dr. Brigid Dwyer—'

'Can we call you Brigid?' Nudge interrupted. 'Brigid's a neat name.'

'Yes, of course,' said Dr. Dwyer. 'We're pretty informal around here.'

'I'm Melanie Bone,' said another woman. 'The communications specialist.' She had the sun-streaked, tan look of someone who spent a lot of time outdoors.

The others were introduced as Brian Carey, dive specialist; Emily Robertson, eco-paleontologist; Sue-Ann Wong, ice specialist, whatever that was; and Paul Carey, ship's captain (and brother of Brian), navigator, and expert in South Polar wildlife. They all seemed nice, but they all had a scientist's rabid curiosity, and I felt their eyes boring into us as if making us into Swiss cheese.

'Okay,' I said, standing up. I gauged the width of the room—about fifteen feet, just barely enough. 'Let's just get this out of the way.'

I looked behind me to make sure there was space, then rolled my shoulders and unfolded my wings slowly, trying not to whap anyone on the head. The scientists stared at me, transfixed, as my wings stretched out farther and farther. Nudge ducked as one passed over her head, and then they were mostly extended, almost fourteen feet across.

I must say, I do have pretty wings. They're a lighter brown than my hair, but not as tawny as Nudge's. My primary feathers, the big ones along the bottom outside edges, are streaked with black and white. The secondaries are streaked white and brown. On the undersides of my wings, the covert feathers are a soft ivory color. And over the tops and down the backs of my wings, I have shiny, strong brown feathers fading perfectly into the primaries.

My wings kick butt.

'So they're not connected to your arms,' Melanie Bone said unnecessarily.

I shook my head. 'Nope. We have six limbs.'

'Like dragons,' Nudge said helpfully. I grinned at her.

'Like insects,' said the Gasman.

'They're so big,' said Emily Robertson. 'They're beautiful.'

'Thanks,' I said, feeling self-conscious. 'They have to be big because we're bigger and heavier, proportionally, than birds.'

'How much do you weigh?' Paul Carey

looked as though he wanted to take notes. Then he winced. 'Sorry, I mean—'

'A bit less than a hundred pounds,' I answered. 'The reason I don't look like a skeleton is that our bones and muscles are made differently, lighter. So even though I'm five-eight, I look slender at ninety-seven pounds but not grotesquely skinny.'

They nodded.

'Do you identify as a human or as a bird?' Brigid asked.

No one had ever asked me that before. 'I don't know,' I said slowly. 'I look in the mirror and see a girl. I have hands and feet. But when I'm up in the sky, and the ground is far below . . . I feel my wings working, and I know I can get oxygen out of thin, high air . . . it doesn't feel very . . . human.'

Which is pretty much the most unguarded, touchy-feely, heart-on-my-sleeve thing I'd ever said. I folded my wings in as my face flushed. I felt naked and stupid, and wished I'd kept my big mouth shut. Cheeks burning, I slumped down in my chair, not looking at anyone.

'I feel more human, I think,' Nudge said cheerfully. 'I like clothes and fashion and doing my hair. The stuff I like is what kids like, what people like. Music and movies and reading. I mean, I never want to make a nest for myself or anything.'

We all laughed, and for once I was relieved

at Nudge's chattiness.

'I don't feel all that human,' said Angel, looking thoughtful.

Fang tapped my leg with his foot under the table, as if to say, There's a surprise.

'I'm not sure what I see when I look in the mirror,' Angel went on. You have to remember that she was only six. 'When I think of me, I picture someone with wings. I know I'm not normal. There aren't any kids to hang out with who are like me. Besides the flock. I know I don't fit in anywhere.' She turned big blue eyes on Michael, who was gazing at her intently. 'This world isn't set up for people like me, like us.' She gestured to include the rest of the flock. 'Nothing in this world is designed for us, designed to make us comfortable. We always stick out, we always make do. People want us, or want us dead, because of *what* we are, not *who* we are. It's hard.'

The room was silent. The grown-ups had stricken looks on their faces, like they actually cared. It was pretty heartbreaking, to think of a little kid like Angel having those kinds of feelings. No one knew what to say.

Except Total.

'Not to be pushy,' he said, 'but is there any way to get some chow in this place? I'm starving.'

CHAPTER THIRTY-ONE

Apparently their briefing had not mentioned the talking dog. Even Akila seemed surprised, cocking her head to one side and looking at Total.

We kids just sat there, since we were, unfortunately, all too used to hearing Total talk.

'A sandwich would be nice,' Nudge said, breaking the silence.

'Yes, of course,' said Melanie Bone, recovering from her shock.

Twenty minutes later, we were scarfing down sandwiches and watching a PowerPoint presentation about global warming.

'Global warming is probably the most significant disaster modern society has had to face,' said Sue-Ann Wong.

'Clearly she hasn't seen this season's platform wedges.' Total sniffed. I nudged him with my elbow.

'If mankind continues with its current energy-use habits, there's a probability that sea levels could rise by up to twenty feet within a hundred years,' Emily Robertson added.

'So we'll all have beach houses?' Gazzy asked. 'Cool!'

Paul Carey shook his head. 'Not cool. It

means that most countries will lose a lot of coastal land, plus the wildlife and ecosystems that flourish there. Many states and countries will be smaller, which means more people moving inland. We would lose big parts of Florida, Louisiana, and Texas, and a lot of the eastern seaboard. They would be mostly under water. So tens of millions of people would be displaced, needing new homes, new jobs.'

Huh. Was it really that bad? Maybe they were overreacting. I mean, how could it possibly be that bad if the earth was *one degree* warmer? It just seemed as if the whole world would become like Hawaii or the Bahamas. Fabulous places. Wouldn't we be able to grow more food if there were more warmer places? How much wheat were we harvesting in Siberia?

'What the heck is global warming?' Iggy asked.

'Basically, it's a buildup of certain gases, like carbon dioxide, in our atmosphere,' said Melanie. 'The earth's atmosphere traps them there, and they act like a blanket. It's making the average temperature of the oceans and the air slowly rise.'

'A gas blanket,' said Iggy. 'Well, you should know all about that, Gaz.'

The Gasman grinned, in no way embarrassed.

'It would be nice if the world were a little

warmer,' Nudge said. 'I hate cold weather.'

'Yeah,' said Gazzy. 'No more jackets, no more frostbite, no more car wrecks on icy roads. People would save money by not heating their houses. We could wear shorts all the time.'

That's what I was talking about!

Emily smiled. 'If it were really like that, it might not be too bad,' she said. 'Though I like cold weather and I would miss skiing. But the problem is that one little change in the earth's temperature causes all sorts of other changes. Like falling dominoes.'

'Besides the catastrophic loss of land all over the world, even a slight temperature rise causes more extreme weather everywhere,' Paul explained. 'We already have more hurricanes, tornadoes, tsunamis, earthquakes, and rainfall just because the earth's temperature has risen barely more than a degree in the last hundred years. On the other hand, we have more droughts and more wildfires as well.'

The slide show had pictures of Indonesia after its tsunami, and the Gulf Coast of Louisiana and Mississippi after Hurricane Katrina. We saw pictures of deserts where there had once been crops, and lots of dead cattle and horses and fish whose water had dried up. But hadn't stuff like that happened in every century? The earth had never been totally calm and perfect. There were hurricanes and floods and droughts thousands of years ago, *before* all this global warming stuff.

'The rising temperature affects crops and plants everywhere,' said Brigid Dwyer. 'Trees are germinating an average of ten days earlier. Plants everywhere are blooming earlier. Plants that need cooler weather are slowly moving northward. Plants that thrive in warmer temperatures are more widespread than ever.'

Again, I wasn't sure why this was a problem. Ten days was a tiny amount of time.

'And that's bad because . . .?' Total put his paws on the table. 'Can I have a Coke or something?'

'Don't give him soda,' I said quickly. 'He'll be hiccupping all night.'

'We don't have any soda,' said Michael apologetically, as Total glared at me. 'Just water, milk, tea, or coffee.'

'It's a problem because plants affect animals, and animals affect plants, and the whole system goes out of balance,' Melanie explained.

' "It's the ciiirrrcle of liiiiffffe," ' Iggy sang.

'Scientists estimate that at least two hundred sixty different species are already responding to global warming by changing their migration and reproduction patterns,' Sue-Ann said. 'The loss of plant and animal life can't be calculated.'

Fang had been silent this whole time. Now he spoke. 'But what does this have to do with *us?*'

Which was, of course, the important question.

CHAPTER THIRTY-TWO

'Frankly, you have unique abilities,' said Brigid in response to Fang's question. 'The Antarctic is an unpredictable and dangerous place, but someone who can fly to safety can take greater risks.'

'But we don't know anything about science,' I said. 'Or not much, anyway. I mean, we can hack into computers. We know all kinds of other stuff. But we don't know anything about global warming or the Antarctic.' Or about any of a million things they taught in *schools,* say.

Brigid smiled, and I thought again how young she looked. She *was* a doctor, right?

'That's okay,' she said. 'You don't need to become experts overnight. We have some specific jobs we can teach you to do.'

'But that's not the only reason you're here,' said Brian Carey, speaking up for the first time. 'The truth is, you guys are very newsworthy. As soon as you surface, people take note, and you get into all the newspapers. So who better to get the message out to the world?'

'And what message would that be?' Fang asked quietly, looking at Brigid.

'That our government needs to take global warming seriously,' she said directly to Fang. 'That we need to develop alternative fuel sources, right now. That we need to slash our emissions of greenhouse gases. Plus, we need to do all we can to slow down the extinction by the year 2050 of more than a million species of animals, insects, and plants.'

'What if we don't believe all that stuff?' I asked, and Melanie drew back and blinked. Had the file on me not mentioned my whole 'uncooperative' thing?

'We won't ask you to do anything you don't believe in,' she said sincerely. 'If, after working with us, you don't think what we're doing is worthwhile, then you're free to leave, and you don't have to publicize our cause.'

'You're free to leave at any time,' Brigid said quickly. 'The only reason you're here is that Dr. Valencia Martinez recommended you. I took a course from her when I was getting my doctorate, and we've kept in touch. She called me a few days ago.'

That made sense. I still got a little thrill every time I realized that Dr. Martinez was my *mom*. That would never wear off.

'Okay,' I said. 'We need to think about this and talk it over; me and the flock, I mean.'

'Of course,' said Michael. 'Let us know if you need any more information. Are you guys still hungry?'

'We're always hungry,' said Nudge.

'We need between three thousand and four thousand calories a day,' I explained. 'When it's *warm.*'

The scientists unsuccessfully tried to hide their surprise.

'Um, well, let's see what we can rustle up,' said Brigid, leading the way to the galley.

'Thanks,' said Fang. 'Appreciate it.'

I watched him follow her out the door, his dark head maybe six inches higher than hers. She looked back at him and smiled, and that's when I got an icky feeling in the pit of my stomach.

CHAPTER THIRTY-THREE

Let me tell you, it was *cozy* in the tiny galley, which was so small that Fang had to totally squeeze in next to Brigid on the bench. Just too freaking cozy for words.

Beneath Gazzy and Nudge's excited chatter, I could follow the low undercurrent of Fang and Brigid playing the get-to-know-you game.

'You're young to be a doctor,' he said, helping himself to a fourth sandwich.

'I'm twenty-one,' Brigid admitted. 'Sort of whizzed through MIT, then got my doctorate at the U of Arizona.' She paused, thinking. 'In a way, I understand what it feels like to stick out, to be different from everyone else. I finished high school when I was twelve.' She gave a self-conscious laugh. 'People called me a freak. Even my parents didn't know what to do with me.'

'That must have been rough,' Fang said sympathetically, while my eyes widened.

'Max?' Melanie was holding out a carton. 'Would you like some milk?'

'*Gross,* no,' I said without thinking. 'I mean, no, thank you. But Gazzy probably would. He likes it.'

'How old are *you?*' Brigid asked Fang.

I almost gagged on my potato chip.

'Fourteen. I think,' Fang said. 'None of us are real sure of our birth dates. But we think Max, Iggy, and I are around fourteen.'

'You seem older,' Brigid murmured, and I shot to my feet, unable to bear this a second longer.

'I need some air,' I managed to get out between swallows.

I felt everyone looking at me as I bolted out of the galley and up the stairs to the deck.

'Max? Are you okay?' Sue-Ann called after

me, but I didn't answer. Instead I ran down the deck of the boat, feeling its engines churning beneath my feet. Just as I was about to slam into the metal side railing, I jumped out over the water and unfurled my wings. I stroked hard, down and then up, over and over, rushing into the cold night sky. Seconds later the *Wendy K.* was just a tiny steam-emitting dot on the blackness of the ocean, and I felt like I could breathe again.

Okay, Max, what's going on? For once the voice in my head was my own. I didn't answer it. Instead I just wheeled through the sky, catching the occasional updraft and coasting. I breathed in and out deeply, thinking about this mission, thinking about Fang and Brigid, and Fang and me, and me and the flock.

I almost forgot to keep checking all around me for Flyboys. Almost.

Maybe a month ago, my mom had taken a computer chip out of my arm. (She's a vet. How appropriate.) I'd been all dopey on anesthesia, and I'd said some stupid stuff to Fang. He'd thrown it back in my face several times since then. And lately he'd kissed me a couple times, and I didn't know where he was going with that. I was torn between (1) wanting to give in, to just let those emotions flood out and see what happened between us, and (2) sheer terror.

Now he seemed to be making cow eyes at a

doctor who was seven years older than him.

And the one thing that stood out in my mind as I wearily made my way back down to the boat in ever-diminishing circles was:

Fang had never said that stupid stuff back to me.

CHAPTER THIRTY-FOUR

When I got back to the boat, all seven scientists were waiting on the deck. Three of them had night-vision binoculars trained on me. I made a short running landing and pounded to a stop. I walked toward them with my wings still outspread, letting them cool off.

'What's up?' I asked with a sudden clutch in my heart. *Had something happened? Had the boat been attacked? Was the flock okay?* I thought I'd kept it in my line of sight, but I knew that I'd been so wrapped up in my own personal soap opera I could have missed Shamu leaping over the boat with a red ball in his mouth.

'We were just . . . watching,' Paul Carey said softly.

'Is something wrong?' I pressed.

'No, no, nothing's wrong,' said Melanie quickly. 'We just—we've never seen anyone fly before.'

'Oh. No, I guess you haven't.'

'Is it . . . wonderful?' Melanie asked.

Again we were treading close to personal ground, and I was feeling all self-protecty, but I answered. 'Yes. The flying part is wonderful. Better than anything.' Growing up in dog crates, being subjected to horrible experiments, being chased and attacked every time we turned around: not so much.

'I wish—' said Brigid. She stopped and shook her head.

'What?'

She looked embarrassed. 'I'm a wildlife specialist, like Paul. I'm here to learn about South Polar animals. The scientist in me is dying to ask you questions, to learn what it's like to be such a different form of human. But I know how awful that must seem to you.'

I bit my lip so I wouldn't say something snide, like, 'Why don't you ask Fang?'

'You're human, with intelligence, courage, feelings, impressions,' Brigid went on. 'I can't ask a bird how it feels to fly. I can ask you. But your very ability to tell me means that asking you such a thing would be horribly intrusive and insensitive on my part. I'm sorry.' She gave a little smile. 'I'll try to keep a lid on the scientist in me.'

'Good luck with that,' said Paul, chuckling. 'Being a scientist isn't what you *do*. It's what you *are*.'

Brigid nodded, looking troubled.

These people were unlike most other humans I'd ever dealt with. They were just as curious, but they were actually respecting our personal boundaries—for now. Most other scientists were content to trap us, slap us into cages, and start sticking needles into us. It was weird. I wondered how long it would last.

'I'm going to turn in,' I said abruptly, and headed toward the aft stairs. (*Aft* means 'rear' on a boat. See how I'm throwing the lingo around?)

I had just started down the narrow, steeply pitched steps when I realized Fang was waiting for me at the bottom.

'What's the matter with you?' he asked. 'Why'd you take off like that?'

Oh, like I would tell *him*.

'Wanted some air,' I said, trying to brush past him. But he took my arms to hold me in place, and because I didn't feel like having this escalate into a knockdown fistfight, I let him.

'Tell me what's going on,' he said again, his face very close to mine.

'Nothing.' I'm nothing if not stubborn.

'Max, if you would just talk to me—'

'About *what?* You and me? There *is* no you and me. Especially when you keep throwing yourself at everything in a skirt!' Okay, now, that was so, so stupid. Fang's eyes widened— I'd given far too much away. Plus, Brigid

Dwyer wasn't wearing a skirt.

I wrenched my arms away from him, feeling as if my cheeks were on fire. I was confused and miserable—two of my least favorite things.

'You're wrong, Max,' he said in a low, dark tone that made butterflies in my stomach. 'There's a you and me, all right. There will always be a you and me.'

I pushed past him, hard, and tried not to run for the room Nudge, Angel, and I were sharing.

CHAPTER THIRTY-FIVE

'Max!'

I was assaulted by excited bird kids as soon as I stepped over the threshold. Iggy and Gazzy were sitting on our bunks, and there was so much energy in the air that we could have powered the boat with it.

'Yeah?' I said, trying to calm my jangled nerves.

'Max, this is great!' said Nudge. 'This is way better than going to school. Or being on the run. It's like we have something fun to do, *plus* we have people protecting us, *plus* food and beds, all at the same time!'

'The food and beds are a huge plus,' I agreed.

'And we have a real mission,' said Gazzy. 'I mean, you've *been* having a mission. But now we're in on it too. And it's a good mission!'

'You think?' I looked for a place to sit down and finally chose the tiny chair at the tiny built-in desk as my only option. Total was stretched out on Angel's bunk, not sleeping, just sighing heavily from time to time.

'Yeah, I think!' said Gazzy.

'It's pretty cool,' said Iggy. 'Despite being cooped up like sardines in this can. It still makes sense. I'd like to do some actual good, instead of just trying to thwart bad all the time.'

'What's wrong with *him?*' I jerked a thumb at Total just as Fang joined us. I didn't look at him and was furious to feel my cheeks heat up again.

Angel patted Total's small black head. 'I think it's Akila,' she confided.

'Cruelty, thy name is woman!' Total moaned. 'Or rather, dog.'

'She won't talk to him,' Gazzy told me.

'Total, she doesn't talk,' I pointed out.

'She won't even talk to me in the *universal language,*' Total said.

'French,' Angel said knowingly.

'Love hurts,' Fang said, almost to himself.

'Oh, shut *up!*' I snapped.

Which made five heads swivel toward me. I wanted to spit.

'Let's talk about something interesting,' I said pointedly. Fang + Brigid = pain. Check. Fang + me = confusion, and also pain and fear. Check. Mission to save the world? Scary, challenging, uncertain, possibly very worthwhile. Check.

Total in love with a Malamute? That I could handle.

'What's the problem, Total?'

'She won't give me the time of day,' Total said wearily. 'I can't blame her. Look at her— she's purebred, classy, important. *Tall*. I'm . . . a short mutant with no papers. Always on the run, hanging out with hunted criminals—'

'Hey!' I said.

'You've stolen three cars,' Total pointed out. 'That I know of. Plus breaking and entering, assault—'

'Okay, okay,' I said irritably. 'Whatever. Hey, anytime it's too much for you, pal . . .'

Angel wrapped her arm around his neck.

Total drew himself up proudly. 'And leave you on your own? I'm not a traitor! You need me!'

I was about to retort with a scathing 'For *what?*' when Nudge interrupted.

'Total, just be nice to Akila,' she advised. 'Don't grovel. Just be yourself, but extra thoughtful, polite. Act more like a dog, you know, strong and silenter.'

Total seemed to take this in, nodding

114

thoughtfully.

'Now, about the mission,' said Nudge. 'I'm all for it! I mean, it's cold here, which sucks, but I like these people. I say we stay for a while.'

'Me too!' said Gazzy.

They were all waiting for me.

I didn't want to argue with them about jumping on the global warming bandwagon. What the hey. We had food and beds. 'All right,' I said, and they erupted into cheers. 'Let's stay for a while.'

CHAPTER THIRTY-SIX

'You need a jacket,' I told Total the next day. We were on the upper deck, and it was, hey, really cold! The scientists had all sorts of cold-weather gear for us kids, so we were okay. They hadn't even minded us slicing long slits in the backs.

Total was shivering, watching the endless ocean through the metal railings.

'Akila doesn't wear a jacket,' he said through chattering teeth.

'Then go below before I have to chip ice off your nose,' I said.

Turning with great dignity, he trotted over to the stairs and jumped down them.

'I can't get used to a talking dog,' said Melanie, coming up next to me. 'Or even flying kids, really.' She gave me a friendly smile, then went back to making notes in a log.

'What's that?' I asked.

'We document weather conditions every day,' she explained. 'Air temperature, barometric pressure, water temperature. Wind direction and speed, what the seas are like.' She flipped through the pages in her log to show me month after month of meticulously graphed weather conditions. It was cool that *someone* was doing this, but it would have made me gonzo by the fourth day.

'You gotta check out their computers,' Nudge said, running up to us. 'They are so cool! They can show you what the earth will look like in fifty years, or what would happen if there's an earthquake. Gazzy just ran a demonstration of what would happen if a tsunami hit Los Angeles!'

'Cool,' I said. 'What're Fang and Iggy doing?'

'Scalping Brian and Brigid at poker,' she said matter-of-factly. Melanie looked up in surprise.

'What about Angel?'

'She's ahead by about thirty bucks.'

Here's a freebie: Don't play poker with a kid who can read minds. Well, they would have to learn sometime.

116

'How long have you been here?' I asked Melanie out of sheer boredom. I don't usually bother getting to know people, because (a) I don't trust any of them, (b) we're usually leaving soon, and in a hurry, and (c) they're usually trying to kill us. The only humans I'd ever met and liked were my mom and my half sister, Ella.

'I've been part of an Antarctica team for five years,' she said. She put a small plastic container in a clawlike thing, which she lowered over the boat's side on a rope. 'Off and on. We're privately funded, so every once in a while we run out of money and have to scramble.' She looked at me curiously. 'How long have you been on the run? Dr. Martinez warned us we'd have to take extra measures to keep you safe.'

I decided it wouldn't be a disaster to tell her. 'We've been on our own for more than two years. On the run for—I don't know—six months? It feels like forever.'

She nodded sympathetically.

Just then Angel appeared on deck, stuffing a wad of money into her pocket. 'Whales,' she said.

117

CHAPTER THIRTY-SEVEN

'Huh?' I said.

Angel nodded toward the ocean. 'Whales. I wanted to see them.'

Melanie drew up her water sample. 'Yes, we'll probably see some before too long. There are eight different species of whales in this region.'

'We're gonna see 'em *now,*' said Angel, moving to the railing.

Smiling, Melanie said, 'We'll definitely see them at some point.'

'No, they're here,' said Angel, pointing. 'They're curious. They think this boat smells yucky.'

'What?' Melanie said, just as the biggest gol-dang animal I've ever seen suddenly burst out of the ocean.

I gasped—it was like a gray-and-black wall of wet skin, almost filling my vision. It was super close, maybe forty feet away, and it got about two-thirds of its body above water before crashing back down in a ginormous belly flop that rocked our boat.

Angel smiled.

'That was a humpback,' said Melanie. 'They love to throw themselves out of the water. You think he was curious?'

'She,' Angel said absently, watching the water. 'She's curious. There's a bunch of them down there.'

Paul Carey came out of the pilothouse. 'There's a pod of humpbacks all around us,' he said. 'I just saw them on sonar.'

Angel glanced at him pityingly but didn't say anything.

'I can't believe how huge they are. How many of them are there?' I asked Angel.

'Can't tell,' she said slowly. 'They're all thinking at once. Maybe twenty-five?'

Melanie's brow wrinkled, and she looked at Paul, who shrugged.

'There are babies,' said Angel. 'They want to come closer, but their moms are saying no. Their moms know the boat is unnatural and shouldn't be here, but they're mostly curious, not mad or anything.'

Paul looked at Angel. 'Do you like making up stories about things you see?' He sounded friendly, not trying to be insulting.

Angel gazed at him seriously. 'I'm not making things up. Uh-oh.' She turned quickly, and two seconds later, another whale suddenly breached even closer to us, leaping almost entirely out of the water and then crashing down. It looked so, so fun.

'He was showing off,' Angel told me. 'Like a teenager.'

'Are we missing something here?' Melanie

asked. 'I don't understand.'

'I'm not just a weird little kid,' Angel told Paul, whose eyes widened. 'Well, actually, I guess I *am* a weird little kid, but not in the way you're thinking.'

'I'm not thinking—' Paul began, but Angel shook her head.

'My file should have told you,' she explained. 'I can hear what people are thinking.'

I decided not to mention that often she could also *control* what people were thinking.

Angel patted her pocket of poker winnings regretfully, as if realizing she wouldn't be able to pull that again on this crew. 'Not just people, but most animals too. I heard the whales thinking and came up to see them.'

Paul and Melanie were at a loss for words.

Get used to it, I thought.

CHAPTER THIRTY-EIGHT

It was hard having to stay on the *Wendy K.,* taking three days to get from Argentina to Antarctica, when we could have flown it in about five hours. We did go for nice, long flights a couple of times a day. The air was cold, but no colder than it was at 25,000 feet, which was well below freezing. We found out that frigid air didn't bother us as long as we were moving, but standing around on the ship's deck got pretty uncomfortable.

Total broke down and consented to wear a small down dog coat. Akila had worn it as a puppy. During a record-setting cold spell, when it was, like, eighty below zero.

'Land ahoy!' Gazzy shouted from five hundred feet in the air. He pointed into the distance, where I could see a white island sticking up out of the ocean.

Michael Papa squinted at the horizon. 'It should be visible pretty soon,' he said. 'The air is so clear here that we get great visibility.'

'It's visible now,' I told him. 'We have really good eyesight. Like hawks.'

He nodded, digesting this, and again I saw the look of almost envy that I'd seen on all these scientists' faces from time to time. No one had ever been truly envious of our abilities before, and it was a cool feeling. The bird kid version of being a football captain or homecoming queen. Sort of.

'I see gray, like rocks,' I told Michael. 'I thought everything was covered in snow.'

'Virtually everything is,' he said. 'But along the coasts and some of the outer islands, there are thin strips of bare rock where glaciers have broken off. Also, it's summer here now, since the seasons are reversed, so things aren't as icy as they can be.'

121

'I see red buildings.'

'I don't see a thing yet,' Michael said regretfully. 'But, yes, the buildings are usually bright red or bright lime green, to stand out as much as possible.'

'Like if there's a blizzard?'

'Uh-huh. Though here blizzards just mean ferocious winds blowing snow and ice around. Hardly any new snow ever falls. Almost never.'

'That's so weird,' I said.

'What's weird?' Fang asked, making me jump. I hadn't heard him come up behind me, as usual. For the past two days I'd been kind of avoiding him. I'd stood back and watched as he and Brigid Dwyer struck up a mutual-admiration society. She didn't flirt with him, but they hung out together a lot, and every time I saw their heads bent over a computer screen or map, it made my stomach clench. Also my teeth. And my fists.

'That it doesn't snow here,' I said. 'Not a lot of precipitation.'

Fang nodded. 'Brigid says the air here is some of the driest on earth.'

'I guess you'll be glad to get off the boat,' Michael said. 'We'll be staying in the guest quarters at the Lucir station. They get tourists there every year.'

'I didn't realize we'd be around a bunch of other people,' I said slowly. I'd gotten almost—well, *comfortable* is a strong word, but

122

somewhat *less tense,* which is about as good as I ever get—around the scientists on board the *Wendy K.* I didn't want to start over with a bunch of strangers. Especially given the explode-o-pizza in Washington.

'There are twelve permanent families who live and work here,' Michael explained. 'About forty people in all.'

Fang's eyes met mine. Time to be back on guard.

CHAPTER THIRTY-NINE

A Poem

By Max
White is the color of little bunnies with pink noses.
White is the color of fluffy clouds fluffing their way across the sky.
White is the color of soft-serve ice cream in a cone.
White is the color of angels' wings and Angel's wings.
White is the color of brand-new ankle socks fresh out of the bag.
White is the color of crisp sheets in schmancy hotels.
White is the color of every last freaking, gol-

danged thing you see for endless miles and miles if you happen to be in Antarctica trying to save the world, which now you aren't so sure you can do because you feel like if you see any more whiteness—Wonder Bread, someone's underwear, teeth—you will completely and totally lose your ever-lovin' mind and wind up pushing a grocery cart full of empty cans around New York City, muttering to yourself.

That was my first poem *ever.*

Okay, so it's not Shakespeare, but I liked it.

We tied up at the Lucir station's dock, next to a couple other boats. Awaiting us were a bunch of bright red metal buildings built up on stilts.

'They're expecting us,' said Sue-Ann, motioning to the first building. 'We can go in, meet some people, and they'll show us to the guest quarters.'

'Okay,' I said, teeth prepared to clench, prebattle adrenaline starting to trickle into my veins.

There was no green: no trees, no shrubs, no grass, no weeds. There were also no sidewalks, no trash, no skyscrapers, no cars. It was completely different from anything we'd ever seen before, and suddenly the phrase 'polar opposites' made a lot more sense.

'This is like being on the moon,' Nudge said

in an awed voice. 'It's so clean.'

'We're explorers,' said Gazzy happily. 'We might see stuff no one else has ever seen.'

I looked at my flock. Each of them seemed a little nervous and a lot excited. They had a real purpose, beyond just cleaning their rooms or keeping watch or finding food. Even if that real purpose was concocted by scientists to create needless panic in the populace, still. The kids felt as though they could help. Clearly they just wanted to forget that this time three weeks ago we'd been fighting for our lives *again*. And, I mean, why would any kid want to forget *that?*

If they really liked being here, really really liked it, would they still come with me when it was time to leave? Because no matter what happened here or how much they felt they were helping, we would still eventually have to leave. We always leave.

This reality check brought to you by Max. You're welcome.

Fang and Iggy were facing away from the station buildings, in the direction of the endless whitescape. Fang stood out against the ice as if carved out of black marble. He turned and motioned me over with a nod.

'Gosh, lots of . . . white, huh?' I said, bouncing on my heels, already feeling the cold.

'Yeah . . . ,' Iggy said in a weird voice.

'You're actually not missing that much, Ig,' I

told him. 'It's not like other places, where there's tons of different stuff to see. Everything here is pretty much white. Lots of sharp white edges.'

Fang touched my hand, and I turned to him. He nodded at Iggy.

'I know,' said Iggy. 'I can see it.'

CHAPTER FORTY

Okay, I'm going to float out a theory here, and maybe it's crap, but I'm thinking that the complete absence of color had something to do with the blind kid suddenly being able to see stuff.

'Cause he really could. I waved my hand in front of his face, and he blinked and pulled away.

'What are you *doing?*' he asked, frowning.

I let my jaw drop open, looking from him to Fang and back, and then Iggy was smiling huge in a way he hardly ever does, and Fang was grinning in a way he hardly ever does, and I felt like skipping around like a ballerina, which, I promise you, I never, ever do.

'What's going on?' Gazzy asked, coming over to us.

'Iggy can *see,*' I said, still unable to believe it.

Excitedly Iggy whirled to see the Gasman, and then stopped dead, frowning. He blinked several times.

'It's . . . it's gone,' he said in a hollow voice.

'What?'

'You could see?' Gazzy asked.

Iggy turned around again, his head hanging. He sighed heavily, then stiffened. 'No! I can see again! I see the white mountains again!'

So here's the deal: Iggy could see *whiteness*. He could see the shapes of the cliffs and glaciers, the occasional gray rocks jutting out from the snow, the horizon line where land met sky. When he turned around, the ocean, the rocky shore, everything, went blank.

'I'm cold,' I said after we'd been standing around looking at Iggy look at stuff for a while. 'Let's go inside.'

Lucir station consisted of about fifteen metal buildings raised up on steel stilts. Some of them were connected, like stepping-stones, going up the nearest hill. A few stood alone. Most of them had snowcats and bobsleds and ice trucks parked underneath.

We climbed the stairs, and once again Iggy had to rely on touching the hem of my jacket and concentrating on the sounds around him. I could feel him seething with disappointment.

The door of the building opened into an air lock. We took off our jackets and stuff there, then went through another door into the actual station.

We met the scientists who lived and worked at the station, ignoring their curious looks and unspoken questions. They showed us to the guest quarters, which were in a separate metal hut. It was small but cozy and comfortable, with one room full of bunk beds, four high; a small living room; a bathroom; and a tiny kitchen.

'Hey!' said Brigid, knocking on our door. 'You guys want to see some penguins?'

'Yeah,' Iggy muttered bitterly. 'Make 'em stand against a white cliff.'

Fang and I looked at each other. Some of us had had new skills show up lately. Would Iggy's be his eyesight?

And here's another question: When was all our world-saving gonna start?

CHAPTER FORTY-ONE

The Uber-Director's assistant looked up from a computer monitor. 'The mutants have arrived at the station, sir, as expected.'

The Uber-Director couldn't nod, but he blinked. 'They're all together? None of them stayed on the boat?'

'No, sir.' The assistant gestured to his monitor and pressed a button. Instantly the screen showed a somewhat grainy image of the six mutant children trooping across packed snowdrifts toward the Lucir station. The screen split, and the other half showed a still image taken from inside the dining hall of the *Wendy K.* Quickly the assistant zoomed in on the faces of the small group heading inside the station and compared them with close-ups of the faces on the boat. They matched.

'All six are accounted for,' the assistant said.

'Very good,' said the Uber-Director. 'Send a message to our contact, saying that the schedule will continue as planned.'

'Yes, sir,' said the assistant, turning back to his computer.

The Uber-Director sent a thought command, and moments later the door opened. A hulking creature almost seven feet tall and easily over three hundred pounds stepped into the room.

'Ah, Gozen,' said the Uber-Director.

The assistant stiffened in his chair and slowly sneaked a peek. If the soldiers creeped him out, this Gozen thing positively terrified him. Not only was he huge, but he had a human face patched onto a Frankenstein body. A curved, shiny metal plate covered part of his bare skull where they couldn't get skin to grow. One arm was a foot longer than the other, and the hand had metal spikes grafted onto the knuckle bones. His other arm, tinted faintly greenish as if the circulation had never worked properly, was hugely veined and muscled, the result of injecting human growth hormone directly into the flesh.

The face was human, but when the creature spoke, you could clearly see the bolts in his jawbone right beneath the skin. Just the other day, the assistant had seen Gozen reach out, snatch a songbird from the air, and casually break its neck, tossing the light, brightly colored body aside. The assistant didn't know whether Gozen had morals or ethics or any sense of right or wrong. Mostly what he had been given was extreme, astonishing power.

'Gozen,' the Uber-Director said again as the hulking thing stood near him, at attention. 'It's almost time. Prepare your troops.'

'Yes, sir,' Gozen said without moving. His voice sounded like a tape of a human voice played too slowly.

A chill went down the assistant's back.

CHAPTER FORTY-TWO

As it turned out, all the world-saving started the next day.

Now, someone who doesn't know better might think that playing with penguins wouldn't really do a lot to prevent the apocalypse, but hey, we were just there to help.

'Look at this! I'm a penguin!' Angel yelled, flinging herself onto her stomach and sliding down a steep, hard-packed snow slope. She raced incredibly fast toward the bottom, where about twenty emperor penguins waited for her, flapping their wings.

'Me next!' Gazzy didn't wait for Angel to get out of the way, he just threw himself down the slope, cackling maniacally. He collided with her, of course, causing her to skid into a few penguins who, frankly, should have been paying more attention. Two of the big heavy birds went down, one right on top of Gazzy. I heard his breath whoosh out from where I was standing, taking scientific notes.

Here's a sample of my contribution to the world's scientific knowledge.

Place: Lucir station, Antarctica

Date: Remind me to check and fill in later

Time: Hard to tell, what with the midnight sun and all, and I hocked my watch ages ago

Subjects: Emperor penguins

Quantity: Twenty-seven adults—no way to tell at a glance who's male or female, and I ain't checking under their hoods. Twelve fuzzums little chickums. Five avian-Americans.

Size: These penguins are surprisingly big—

about four feet tall. Solid and heavy, judging from the way Gazzy whoofed when one fell on him. I'd say—sixty pounds? We're talking major birds here.

Birds' condition: They're hefty little suckers, built for comfort *and* speed. And they're sure not feeling the cold. I'd put them on the 'chunky' end of the scale.

Activity: Basically, sliding on ice, just for fun. Leaping into the frigid water every once in a while, then popping back out as if shot from a toaster. Noticeably fishy smell afterward. One barfed up part of an octopus, almost on Iggy's boots. Good thing his vision was out again. I almost heaved myself.

'How's it going?' Brian Carey asked, snowshoeing up to us. He and Sue-Ann, who was with him, had clipboards and special pens that wrote in extreme weather. Did I mention how freaking cold it was? Like, thanks, Mom!

Sue-Ann looked at the penguins popping up out of the water and laughed. 'They're so cute—' she began, as a whole horde of the tuxedoed birds shot up onto the ice. They were squawking and waddling away from the water as fast as they could.

And then suddenly an enormous creature surged out of the ocean, grabbed Sue-Ann by a leg, and sank back into the black depths.

CHAPTER FORTY-THREE

'Leopard seal!' Brian yelled, throwing down his clipboard and racing toward the water. 'Get help! Get Paul and the others!'

Sue-Ann's head bobbed out of the water, and she screamed, but she was choked off as the seal dragged her under again. It was huge, with a watermelon-sized head, its sharp-toothed jaws clamped around Sue-Ann's leg.

'Go!' I ordered Gazzy, who was staring at the water. There were splotches of darkness in the water, and the ice at the opening was faintly tinged with pink. 'Go! And the rest of you, get back to the station!'

Immediately, without question, Gazzy grabbed Iggy, and they, Nudge, and Angel started slipping and running over the snow back to the station. I heard Gazzy yelling for help.

'It'll thrash her around in the water till she's dead!' Brian cried, leaning over the sharp edge of the ice. 'Sue! Hang on!' He looked back toward the station helplessly, and then shouted and waved his arms as the seal surfaced again.

He couldn't jump in—he'd get sucked beneath the ice and never find his way out. Or the leopard seal would get *him.*

'Come on!' I told Fang, and ran to a quick takeoff. He was right behind me, and we stayed low, swooping over the water, trying to see. A dark shadow almost ten feet long showed that the seal was still close to the surface.

'Grab her as soon as it comes up again,' I shouted, and Fang nodded, grimly determined. Together we flew low, six feet above the water, in tight circles, ready to pounce in a second. Already a rescue team was rushing toward us. Paul was carrying a harpoon.

'There!' I said, pointing. The shadow was growing darker, then, sure enough, the seal surfaced again, Sue-Ann still gripped in its jaws. She was limp, her eyes closed, but instantly Fang and I swooped down, dropping toward the water like hail.

Fang kicked the seal's eel-like head as hard as he could with his heavy boot, and I brought both feet down on its sleek, arched back. It recoiled in surprise, opening its jaws for a split second, rearing to look at us. It gave a huge, awful roar, looking like a sea monster, but Fang and I had already grabbed Sue-Ann's jacket and one arm, and we were stroking our wings downward with great effort, trying to get aloft. The seal roared again and snapped, narrowly missing my feet, and I pulled them up.

Then we were out of danger's range and flying over land. We held Sue-Ann tightly, bypassing the astonished rescue team and heading straight to the infirmary building. We skidded to a clumsy landing, sliding on the ice, Sue-Ann's wet jacket already frosting over with ice crystals. I didn't even know if she was still alive, or if we had just rescued a body. Her pants were torn and blood soaked.

Two men rushed out of the infirmary with a stretcher and placed it on the ice next to Sue-Ann. One placed his fingers on her neck, feeling for a pulse, while the other prepared to lift her carefully onto the stretcher. Then he frowned. 'What—what's that?'

By this time, some of the others had circled around us. One of the infirmary guys gently touched Sue-Ann's leg where it had been shredded by the seal. He moved her torn pants aside, and then Paul sucked in his breath. My eyes narrowed. Beneath the torn and bloody flesh, we saw a collection of wires and fiber-optic cables embedded deep within Sue-Ann's leg.

'What the heck is that?' Paul demanded. 'Does anyone know about this?'

The other infirmary guy looked up. 'I got no pulse here, chief. She's gone.'

Then the other scientists ran up, out of breath.

'Is she alive?'

'I can't believe what you did!'

'That was amazing! Thank you so much!'

Their faces fell as they saw our expressions, and we stepped back so they could see Sue-Ann. I saw confusion and shock on each face. Unless they were dang good actors, none of them had known that Sue-Ann had been modified. That instead of being one of us, she'd probably been one of Them.

Paul looked up at us, dismay in his eyes. He nodded over at the other members of his team. 'Brian. Get Sue-Ann's computer. Search her quarters.'

'Oh, no,' said Melanie, tears forming in her eyes.

'You all,' Paul said, gesturing to us, 'get inside, out of sight. You others—search the rest of the *Wendy K.*, the guest quarters here, the mess hall, anywhere there might be hidden cameras. We've had a traitor among us.'

CHAPTER FORTY-FOUR

As expected, the antifreeze additive to their joint lubrication proved effective. Gozen gave the signal for the rest of the troops to offload, telling his internal counting program to register whether they were all here.

One by one, the soldiers stepped evenly

down the metal ramp that led from the plane's belly to the hard-packed snow. Their feet adjusted to the new surface instantly, springs and weights compensating for the slipperiness and slight give of the icy land cover.

All the troops were accounted for.

First, a small shelter. The plane's crew had thrown their supplies out onto the ice, and now the ramp closed, and the plane's engines whined.

'Find the shelter,' Gozen ordered three of the soldiers. 'Erect it.'

They responded instantly, locating the large crate strapped with plastic rope. Untying the rope, they pulled the self-inflating, insulating TempHut from the crate. With a couple of cord pulls, the TempHut unfolded and sprang almost comically into a fully inflated shelter, like a jack-in-the-box.

Without a sound, the soldiers found the three-foot screws that would tether the shelter to the ice, to keep the structure from blowing away in the intermittent gale-force winds. It had no heat, no windows, no beds. Which was fine. Since the soldiers weren't human, weren't even alive, that was no problem.

The first pair of recon scouts were ready to report.

'Yes?' Gozen's voice wasn't nearly as mechanical as those of Generation K—it had some inflection and a more normal tone.

'There's a problem,' a scout reported. 'One of our contacts has been damaged. She has sent no signal for the past five hours. Surveillance tapes show that she was attacked. She is presumed dead.'

Gozen considered. In all likelihood, the plan could continue. First, a report to the Uber-Director, detailing what he could find out about their contact. Then he would sit back and wait for the right opportunity. It shouldn't take long.

His job was to eliminate the dangerous mutants. The Uber-Director hadn't specified how. Or how long he could take doing it. Or how much pleasure he could get from it.

All those things were up to him.

'Get into the shelter,' Gozen told his troops.

CHAPTER FORTY-FIVE

You are reading Fang's Blog. Welcome!
You are visitor number: 545,422

Today's theme: Weirdness at the bottom of the world.

Our lives are pretty freaking weird already—what with the wings, the fleeing for our lives, etc. And yet we can still be amazed when things get even weirder. Cool.

Some stuff has kept life interesting for us lately: (1) Iggy can see, off and on. He needs to be practically snow-blinded for it to kick in, but he's actually seen stuff. Made Max wish she'd brushed her hair sometime in the last month. (2) We've flown with snow petrels. They're beautiful white birds, about pigeon size, that are all over the place here. They're like flying pureness, to sound stupid and goofy. If Angel were an actual 100 percent bird, she'd be a snow petrel. The Gasman would be an emu. (3) There have been some penguin incidents, caused by uncautious belly-sliding down packed-snow slopes. Did you know that a penguin, if startled, might suddenly barf on you? We didn't either. Did you know how revolting regurgitated, half-digested krill and squid is? I do now. (4) We performed a daring rescue at sea, made possible by Max and yours featherly. Unfortunately, the person we rescued turned out to be a mole who's probably been spying on us for the past week. So now we're most likely in mortal danger, as per usual.

Fortunately, the person we rescued didn't make it. So I'm guessing her reports have slowed way down. In the meantime, whoever's out there planning God knows what, we're onto you. We see you coming. We're not going to take it well.

I'll go ahead and tell you: We're in

Antarctica. We're here checking out the signs of global warming. Global warming may *sound* comfy—no more winter coats—but everything on earth right now kind of desperately relies on the climate staying *as is.* But if we give up our childish fears of catastrophic flooding, earthquakes, tsunamis, untold plant and animal extinctions, droughts, famines, and whatnot, we could just relax right now and let 'er rip!

However. For those of us who prefer the planet relatively undisastered, it seems clear that things have to change. I mean, we *humans* have to change our habits, our recklessness, our dependence on fossil fuels and beef.

Any questions?

Ali, Ju-Ju, Ariel, and Robin Bernstein from Palm Beach write:
Wassup up with no beef? No hamburgers?

Well, Ali, Ju-Ju, Ariel, and Robin Bernstein, Good thing you asked. For myself, I'm totally about the burgers. And steak. Shish kebabs. Stew. You name it, if it's cow, it's for me.

But this incredibly cool scientist I know, Dr. Brigid Dwyer, told me that livestock is causing more damage to the earth's climate than cars. All the cars. For one thing, cattle 'release' more methane and other

greenhouse gases than even the Gasman, which is saying something. Plus, cattle eat about fourteen pounds of grain to produce one pound of meat. Which is energy efficiency in reverse. Not to mention the deforestation for their grazing land, the water they consume. It all adds up hugely. Makes ya think, huh?
 —Fang

BitterGummy from Honshu writes:
Get off ur soapbox, man! When I want a lecture, I'll go 2 school!
Sounds like you need it, BitterGummy. Try to stay awake this time.
 —Fang

MinkyPuddin from Sydney writes:
Fang I miss u guyz so much. U haven't bin in the newz lately. I am all worried.
 Your #1 fan.

No worries, MinkyPuddin. We're fine. More fine than we've been in a long time, actually.
 —Fang

Shy Babe from Seattle writes:
Dear Fang, I wrote u last month. Do u have a girlfriend?

I recommend you stick to your own species, Shy Babe. Thanks anyway.
— Fang

Okay, guys, gotta go. Global disaster to document, scientists to talk to. And it's dinnertime. I'm guessing it's not beef.
— Fang

CHAPTER FORTY-SIX

'Where are we going?' Nudge asked as we took off into the clear, crisp air.

'Just getting an overview of the area,' I explained. 'A little recon. See what's out here.' Since Sue-Ann's death had revealed her to be a Bad Guy, I'd been extra cautious. Now we were gonna do a little looking around, in case we saw, like, a big trailer with 'Bad Guys' written on the roof.

Fang was silent, flying a bit off by himself. I angled my left wing slightly and swooped closer to him. Things between us were still weird. I missed the old days, when our relationship was simple: each of us totally dedicated to constantly one-upping the other. That, I could understand.

'So I guess we can assume that Sue-Ann was sending updates of our whereabouts to someone,' I said.

He nodded. 'Brigid's trying to hack into her computer for more info.'

There was that name again. 'Nudge should do it,' I said, trying not to show irritation.

'Yeah—if Brigid can't get in, we'll have Nudge take a whack at it,' he agreed.

'Can we go over the islands?' Gazzy called to me. 'There's a volcano in the middle of one! In fact, the whole island is the volcano.'

'Sure.' We arced smoothly in a huge circle to the left, heading away from the enormous continent of ice. It felt great to stretch my wings and suck in the cold, cold air.

'I can't see anything,' Iggy said, sounding depressed.

'Maybe I could ride with Fang?' Total suggested, squirming nervously in Iggy's arms.

'I can still *fly*,' Iggy said irritably. 'I can still *navigate*.'

'Oh, so cool!' Gazzy shouted, pointing.

We'd left the peninsula behind and now were over an island shaped like a raggedy Cheerio with a tiny slit in one side. We began a long series of descending loops toward the island. We all kept our eyes open but saw no one else around.

'That water in the middle is where the volcano blew up,' Gazzy explained.

We got closer and closer. It seemed about as safe as any place could be.

'Thermal!' I said, feeling myself pass through a column of heavier, warmer air. It felt incredible, a pocket of warmth in the middle of the frigid air around us.

'Something's bubbling below,' Angel said, looking down.

'Let's check it out,' I said in my leaderly way.

We went lower, not seeing anyone else, and then landed on a moonscape of fine gray grit, small stones, a bunch of signs, and, oddly, a field covered with what looked like broken wooden barrels. It was unlike anything I'd ever seen before.

And soon it could all be gone.

So, you're back, I thought to the Voice. *Glad you could join us. Okay, maybe not glad, exactly—*

Pay attention, Max, said the Voice. *Memorize what you're seeing. This place might not be here much longer.*

So I guessed the Voice was on board with the whole global warming thing. I said, 'Watch where you step, guys. Don't get scorched by a geyser or anything.'

'There aren't any geysers here,' said Nudge. 'But steam is boiling up through the water.'

'There's been a lot of people here,' said Fang. He stood in front of one of the many signs, in about eight languages, that warned us to be careful, to watch where we stepped, to

144

not destroy any lichen or moss, to not litter, and so on. It was a protected spot, overseen by 'the Deception Island Management Group.'

'Deception Island,' I said, smiling. 'What a cool name. It sounds like where we should live.' I looked around at the surreal, unearthly place. 'If we wanted to live in a barren wasteland.'

' 'S not barren,' said Angel.

Nudge began pulling off her boots.

'What are you doing?'

She pointed to the edge of the water, where steam was misting heavily upward. 'Hot bath! Those dinky little showers back at the station ain't cutting it.'

'Look,' said Angel, pointing upward. I heard them before I saw them: a flock of really big birds, coming off a cliff about a quarter-mile away.

'What are they?' I asked.

'Wandering albatrosses,' said Nudge, who had now shucked her coat and scarf and was peeling down to her underwear. 'Sailors used to think they held the souls of dead sailors. Oh, my God, this water feels fantastic!' She sank down slowly, seeming to almost disappear into the mist.

'Be careful,' I said. 'The water might suddenly turn boiling or something.'

'I'm going in too,' said Total, trotting over to the water.

The albatrosses wheeled overhead. The biggest ones had wingspans bigger than Angel's—maybe nine feet across. They were amazing. They hardly ever flapped their wings—just glided on the rising currents of warm air. Because our body-weight-to-wingspan ratio was so much greater, we probably couldn't pull that off.

'Oh, my God!' Nudge said again, sounding alarmed.

I whipped my head around and hurried toward her. 'What?' Behind me, Fang was examining the sky, the sea, the land, for approaching threats. I skidded to a halt at the water's edge, scattering grit and tiny pebbles. 'What's wrong?'

Nudge pointed at Total. He was up to his nose in the warm water, looking more cheerful than I'd seen him in a long time. His black fur was wet and slicked down against his sides. I peered at what Nudge was pointing at.

'What?' said Total sleepily, relaxing in the steamy water. 'Man, this is heaven on my paws. They get so cold. . . . Maybe little boots . . .'

Now all of us were at the water's edge, frowning at Total.

He groggily blinked up at us. 'You gotta try this. If I had a martini right now, I'd never come out.'

Then it hit me, what I was looking at. I don't know why it took me so long—I'd seen stuff just like it a bunch of times, and not only on us. I somehow never expected it to happen to Total, that's all.

Fang raised his eyebrows. I made a 'Holy moly' face back at him.

'What?' said Total, waking up a bit, realizing we were all staring at him.

I swallowed. 'Uh, Total? You're growing wings.'

I knew there was something strange about that dog, mused the Voice.

CHAPTER FORTY-SEVEN

'Okay,' said Michael Papa the next morning. 'Let's go over some things.'

We looked up from breakfast warily. I'd felt just a weensy bit guilty about how much the flock was eating until the station commander had dropped the info that they allowed between 4,000 and 5,000 calories per person, per day because of the cold. Unlike ordinary humans, we didn't burn that many more calories in really freezing weather. So we were actually getting enough to eat, and we were wolfing it down.

The really jaw-dropping thing? Total had asked to have his breakfast *in a bowl on the floor*—next to Akila's bowl. Of course, eating

Akila's special cold-weather dog food was out—Total still had waffles with syrup and bacon, and a bowl of coffee with milk and sugar.

'We have to press on with our work, despite Sue-Ann's betrayal. Today you guys will accompany some of the scientists here, do a little exploring,' Michael said. 'But you have to remain extra on-guard.'

I nodded.

'You were helping document the status of our local penguin colony before Sue-Ann was attacked,' Michael went on. 'Today you'll go with Emily and Brigid as they take measurements and examine different ice layers. The chemical concentrations of the ice layers tell us a great deal about the history of the atmosphere in this area.'

'But before we set out, we need to go over some safety issues,' said Brigid.

I tried not to, but I flicked a glance at Fang. His eyes were glued to Brigid, his face friendly and unforbidding. I felt my stomach twist, which made me madder at myself than I was at him.

'Obviously, this is an extreme environment,' Brigid said. 'We do have dangers here, as you have seen. For example, what would you do if you suddenly realized you were lost? A lot of the terrain looks the same.'

'I'd fly up till I could see the station,' I said.

'Then head back to it.'

The scientists looked at me, taken aback. I guess that solution hadn't occurred to them.

'Okay,' said Brigid, nodding slowly. 'That would work. Now, there aren't that many crevasses, but they can be extremely dangerous. If you happen to fall into one—'

'I would fly back out of it?' I suggested.

'Um, yeah,' said Brigid, then heroically pressed on. 'Okay, you know the penguins aren't dangerous, nor are any of the other birds here, though you should stay away from nests. And of course there are no polar bears.'

We nodded. Nudge, Angel, and I had been crushed about the lack of polar bearity.

'But as you saw, leopard seals can on occasion attack,' Brigid went on. 'We recommend staying at least twenty meters away from them at all times. But if you do find yourself confronting one again, I'd recom—'

'Flying away from it?' Really, this was too easy. I was bad.

By this time the flock were suppressing smiles.

'Blizzards,' said Brigid firmly. 'Katabatic winds. Sometimes upward of eighty miles an hour. They blow snow and ice particles around, and it can feel like needles.' She paused, as if waiting for me to say I'd fly out of it.

Which I didn't. You'd have to be a complete

149

moron to fly in a storm like that. Last time I looked, I wasn't a moron.

'Hunker down,' said Brigid, relieved to finally be able to give us advice. 'Dig a hole for yourself in a snowbank. Stay together. Don't eat ice for hydration—it'll only lower your core temperature. Stay put and wait for help. We *will* come find you.'

'Aye aye,' I said, and saluted.

Brigid gave me a faint smile, and then we all suited up to brave the great outdoors. Brian Carey watched us gather our equipment. He was staying behind to type up some reports.

Ordinarily, Sue-Ann would have taken the ice samples we brought her and put them through her chromatograph. Now it was Melanie's job. She would analyze how concentrations of carbon dioxide and other chemicals had changed through the centuries. Basically, they were finding that carbon dioxide levels—primarily a by-product of burning fossil fuels—were the highest they'd been in the past 800,000 years.

Being completely objective here, I could see how that would seem like a bad thing.

CHAPTER FORTY-EIGHT

'Knowing that there are evil, bloodsucking corporations out there willing to spend a bazillion dollars to create machines whose only purpose is to kill us mutant bird kids is depressing,' said Nudge. We were kneeling on the ice, helping Melanie and Brigid drill their core sampler down into it. 'Knowing there are evil, bloodsucking corporations out there who are knowingly and willingly destroying the only planet we have to live on just to *make* bazillions of dollars is worse.' Nudge sighed and looked bummed.

Okay, I totally admitted that there were evil corporations out there who were complete bad guys and were polluting everything in sight. I got that. But I still wasn't sure that it was all causing global warming, or that having a slightly warmer earth would be that bad.

'How can they possibly stand themselves, knowing what they're doing?' I agreed. 'I mean, how many cute shoes can one company need?' You'd think I was megalomaniacal enough to understand their mind-set, but I didn't. It was like, make a bunch of money so you can control things, like land or armies or governments or countries—and you want to control them so you can . . . essentially make more money. So you can control more things. So you can make more money. Kind of an empty loop, huh?

Not to be judgmental.

But *someone* had to be judgmental! Someone had to *judge* that this was crazy and wrong, and those companies were boneheaded idiots! If that person had to be me, so be it. I might not be the perfect spokesmodel against global warming, but I could still absolutely be against pollution. That had been proven to be bad, beyond a shadow of a doubt.

'I want a baby penguin,' said Angel, tugging on my jacket to get my attention.

She snapped me out of my alarm-clock-of-doom reverie, and I looked down at her.

'No,' I said, before I really processed what she had said.

Her face got that set look I'd learned to dread.

'No,' I said more firmly. 'You already have Celeste and Total. We cannot also have a baby penguin to cart around. Especially when that baby will grow up to be the size of an average third-grader.'

Angel took a deep breath. 'They're so fuzzy and cute,' she began. 'They make little cheeps. There's a bunch here—it wouldn't even cost anything. We could—'

'Angel?' I said. 'Baby penguins eat a regurgitated mixture of partially digested fish,

152

krill, and an oily substance from their fathers' stomachs. Are you willing to eat a bunch of raw fish and krill, and then barf it back up into a baby penguin's cute, cheeping mouth? Like, every hour?' Sometimes my crushing logic astounds even me.

Angel bit her lip. 'Hm,' she said. She straightened her small shoulders and walked away with dignity. Another disaster averted.

Leaving me with only Fang's adoration of Brigid Dwyer to really get stuck in my craw. (What *is* a craw, anyway? I've always wondered.)

I watched as they worked side by side, his dark head almost touching her blond one. They knelt in the snow, and at one point the brilliant scientist couldn't unscrew the lens from her special camera. She needed the help of a superstrong fourteen-year-old bird kid. Her smile when Fang opened it was almost as blinding as all this freaking snow.

Just then, Akila strode by on her way to where Michael was working. She was followed by Total, who had to trot a bit to keep up. I barely heard part of what he was saying.

'I admire a woman with a career,' he said, his breath making puffs in the air. 'I'm very modern that way. Strength is an admirable quality. . . .'

The back of my neck twitched. Standing up, I cast a hard 360 all around us, shading my eyes from the intense sunlight. We had to wear sunglasses all the time, even Iggy. The bright sun here, reflecting off the snow and ice, could permanently damage our eyes.

'Max—check it out!' said Nudge as she and the Gasman ran up to me.

I held up one finger, meaning wait.

Something was wrong. The horizon was clear. The sky above and around us was empty. Even using my raptor vision, I couldn't detect anything moving toward us over the ice. I looked again and again, examining the ocean, the land, and the sky. Anything coming at us from any angle would stick out like a pork chop at a vegan convention.

I couldn't see a thing.

But something was wrong. There was a threat somewhere.

The flock was now aware of my unease, including Fang, who immediately stood and looked around himself. Iggy instinctively came closer to the rest of us, moving unerringly over the rugged terrain.

Fang completed his surveillance and raised one dark eyebrow at me. I shrugged and frowned. We both stood still, using all our senses to assess our safety.

'Fang?' asked Brigid. After another look at me, Fang turned and went back to her. I tried to focus on the neat shell Nudge was holding out, and the large tooth of something that the

Gasman had found.

But I could only give them half my attention.

Something was wrong, and sooner rather than later, I would find out what it was.

CHAPTER FORTY-NINE

You are reading Fang's Blog. Welcome!
You are visitor number: 723,989

Yo, faithful readers. You know, when I was a kid, my big ambition was to someday not live in a dog crate. Some kids aim high, I don't know. But here's a thought, for those of you who haven't decided on a big ambition: How about being a scientist?

I know, we all think Bill Nye the Science Guy. Or maybe Dr. Bunsen Burner from that kids' show with the Muppets. But being a scientist (not the evil kind, obviously) can be awesome. I know, because I've met some non-evil scientists recently.

Right now we're working with a bunch of scientists that rock the house. One of them is only a little older than me, and not at all geekified. I have to say, a chick who's super smart and super brave, dedicated to her work, wanting to help people, save the world—well, there's nothing hotter than that.

So if you're not a total wastoid, consider checking out science. We're gonna need all the help we can get to save what's left of the planet. It'll be up to us. We'll need to have some real skills, real tools. Remember my 'Useful Jobs' list from before? There were a lot of jobs on it that could help us in the future. Put down your air guitars, quit pretending to walk down a fashion runway. Go review it.

Slimfan3 from Jacksonville writes:
What about all those guys who were after you?

Well, Slimfan3, either they haven't found us yet, or they all got wiped out. Either way, the past week has been a primo vacation. If you like cold weather.
— Fang

MissLolo from Tulsa writes:
Are you and Max gonna get married anytime soon? <Blushes.>

Uh, MissLolo? We're fourteen years old. We think. Who knows how much longer we'll be around? Who knows where we'll end up? We don't plan more than a day or two ahead.
— Fang

Googleblob from Holy Oak, CA, writes:
Fangalator—
Dude, you are the coolest. I wanna get a tat of your wings on my back. Like, life-size.

Googleblob, unless your back is fourteen feet across, you are out of luck, my friend.
— Fang. Just Fang

S. Haarter from Johannesburg writes:
I really like hearing @ the stuff u r doin to save the planet. U r my hero. I m gonna txt u a pic of me. [pic deleted] I m reading ur blog 2 my science class as my ecology project. Keep it up!
Your #1 fan.

CHAPTER FIFTY

'Fang . . . alator?' I snickered.

Fang shot me a glance, then continued unlacing his polar boots. I couldn't believe he'd written a whole blog about Dr. Amazing and Her Quest to Save the World. I mean, excuse me, but who's been saving the world for the past several months? That would be *me*. Do I get a blog entry? No. Who beat the Omega blockhead, back in Germany? Dr.

Amazing? No.

'You're just mad because I wrote about Brigid,' he said, tugging off a boot, and I pulled back, stung.

'I am not! I don't even read your blog! You can write about whoever you want!'

Fang looked at me. 'You can't have it both ways, Max,' he said. 'You blow me off every chance you get, but then you get mad if I talk to someone else.'

'I do n—' I began hotly, but then realized that was exactly what I did. My face flushed, and I shut my mouth. I didn't even know what we were fighting about.

'You say that like it's a bad thing,' I blustered, but Fang didn't crack a smile.

'I said that we would never split up again,' Fang said, and my heart leaped in panic. 'And I meant it. We have to keep the flock together to survive. But you might want to think about cutting me a break now and then.'

He gave me a last, long look that I could hardly stand, afraid of what I might see in it. Turning, he began to duck out the low doorway when Gazzy raced up, breathing hard.

'I can't find Angel anywhere,' he panted.

'Maybe she's just out flying,' I said.

'She would have told someone,' Gazzy said. 'Total's gone too. Maybe they went walking or something, but it's getting bad out there—

listen to that wind.' He pointed toward the window, and then I realized that the awful wailing and shrieking that I had assumed was just me, panicking inside my head, was actually outside, and weather caused.

We heard voices out in the hall, and then Michael Papa leaned through our doorway. 'Is Akila in here, by any chance? Last I saw, she was outside with Total and Angel, but that was an hour ago. Have they checked in with you?'

Fang's eyes met mine, the tension of a few moments ago completely forgotten.

'Get the others,' I told him, and he nodded. 'Tell them to dress warm.'

CHAPTER FIFTY-ONE

'Well, this sucks big-time,' Total said, and Angel agreed. She swallowed hard and tried to calm down. If Max were here, what would she do? Angel grimaced—Max wouldn't have gotten herself into this situation.

'It's okay,' Total said soothingly to Akila. He turned to Angel. 'Tell her it's going to be okay.'

Angel sent thoughts into Akila's mind. She felt Akila's fear and confusion, but also a tough determination. Akila wasn't prepared to die here. She would do anything to get out.

Us too, Angel told her. *Everything will be okay. We'll get out. Max will come for us. Max always comes for us.* To herself, she thought: *I've got to stop getting into things where Max has to come for me.*

Akila quieted and quit struggling against the ice.

They were probably about a mile from Lucir station. Angel could picture the exact terrain they had crossed, and she could also picture what it would look like from the air. Everything had been fine: They had plenty of time before sunset, she had Total and Akila with her, and there had been a clear trail of penguin tracks for her to follow. All she had wanted to do was get close to a baby penguin—maybe even touch it. If she sent the parents no-harm thoughts, they would probably let her. A baby penguin would feel so soft and downy.

The penguin tracks had led over the snow and ice, and Angel had followed them. Right up until she'd fallen into this crevasse. It had been hidden by hard-packed snow, and the penguins had somehow managed to cross it, though some of them weighed more than Angel. But for some reason, as soon as Angel stepped on it, it had given way. Her wings had flared automatically, pulling up painfully as she slid down deep into the hard, icy crevasse. Yelping and scrabbling frantically, Total and

160

Akila had been sucked down with her.

Now, three minutes later, Angel, Total, and Akila were wedged tightly in a vee made of ice and rock-hard packed snow. Her wings were stuck open, back and behind her, and it really hurt. She tried pulling them in and down but couldn't budge them without feeling like they were going to be ripped out of their sockets.

Worse, Angel feared that below them, the crevasse opened out again, that they were caught in a bottleneck of ice, and if it broke, they would fall down who knew how far. One of her feet was dangling through a crack underneath them, and all she felt around it was cold air. She might be able to catch herself, if she had enough room, but she wouldn't be able to save Total or Akila.

'How far down did we fall?' Total asked.

Angel looked up. 'Um, maybe like . . . eighteen feet? Twenty feet?'

'Maybe if I brace my paws on each side, I can climb up, like a chimney,' Total murmured. 'No—it's too wide at the top. Dang it.' His bright black eyes looked at Angel. 'We goofed.'

'Yeah.' Angel felt guilty—this was all her fault. If she sent a thought, could Max hear it? She didn't think so. It only seemed to work when she was really close to the person.

Akila whimpered and scrabbled again, trying to grab a paw-hold. But she only slipped farther down, and now some of her weight was resting on Angel, pushing her down an inch and making her wings feel an inch more ripped, and her foot an inch more precarious.

Akila, please stop, Angel thought at her. *Calm down and stay very still. We have to think.*

Akila let out a breath. Angel felt her trembling.

Angel's stomach got butterflies when she realized that they wouldn't be visible from the air. Because she wasn't moving, she was starting to feel the horrible grip of coldness seeping under her jacket, her pants. She looked over and saw that both Total's and Akila's whiskers were covered with frost.

Oh, no, she thought with rising panic. *I can't feel my fingers inside my mittens.* This was bad. Surely Max would find them. But until then, Angel had to do what she could to save them herself. What could she do? She was really, really strong. But they were wedged incredibly tightly. She'd already trying pushing with all her might, to unstick her wings, which had now gone numb.

She was really fast, but that didn't help here. She could read people's minds, which helped a little because she calmed Akila down. What else could she do? Well, she could change her looks. Maybe if she changed into her bird of paradise she might be smaller or skinnier and could pull herself out.

Angel closed her eyes and concentrated. She felt herself grow warm, and feeling flowed back into her feet and hands and wings with a thousand burning tingles. She felt the whisper of feathers forming on her face and hands, inside her mittens. She loved the way she looked as a blue bird of paradise. It'd be neat to keep it up all the time. But it took a lot of energy, a lot of concentration.

'Whoa,' Total said groggily, watching her. Angel felt Akila's surprise and sent her calming thoughts. *It's still me.* The transformation was complete, and Angel tried once again to pull herself upward. She pushed down hard with her hands, and though her feathery self was a little smaller, it didn't do anything to help. She was scared to push down with her feet because of the ice maybe breaking away beneath her. Plus she had the weight of Akila on her.

It was no use. Her new skill was worth zilch in this situation. They were going to die here. After everything she had been through, all the times Max had saved her, Max couldn't help her now. Angel had done this to herself. She had killed *herself,* in the end. Tears welled up in her eyes but froze around the rims before they fell.

This was it.

This was the end.

CHAPTER FIFTY-TWO

In the end, I made Gazzy and Iggy stay at the station. They started to give me a hard time about it, but one look at my 'Gonna kill you if you argue' face, and they shut up. They would stay with the scientists and search around the station. Michael and Brigid were taking Nudge with them to search the *Wendy K.,* in case Angel and the dogs had gone back there.

'I don't want you two flying in this storm,' said Paul Carey, looking concerned. 'It's not too bad now, but it's going to get worse. We don't want to have to look for you too.'

I pulled on another pair of socks and jammed my feet into my boots. Fang was looping a coil of climber's rope over his shoulder.

'Max?' Brian said. 'You need to stay here. Let us handle it.' There was an intent tone in his voice that made me glance up at him. He looked worried.

'Guys,' I said, zipping up my parka, pulling the fur-trimmed hood onto my head, 'I take care of my own.'

Paul crossed his arms and took on his ship's-captain persona. 'Max, I forbid you and Fang to go out into that storm!'

I couldn't help chuckling, and Fang cracked

a smile.

We headed to the door that led to the air lock and outside.

Brian stepped between us and the door, and what had been amusing suddenly became irritating.

'Max, you don't know—' he began, and that was when I decked him.

A second later Brian was lying stunned on the floor, one hand to his jaw, blinking and wondering what had happened.

At least I assume that was what he was doing.

I wouldn't know, because Fang and I were already gone.

CHAPTER FIFTY-THREE

Flying in high winds *can* be the most exhilarating thing in the world. You just put your wings fully out and coast, doing micro-adjustments as needed to stay aloft. It's a lot like surfing at the beach, riding the waves, except, you know, without the water. Or the beach. Or the surfboard.

At least, it's fun like that when you don't have to go anywhere and can take all the time in the world to enjoy Mother Nature's roller coaster. If you need to go in *any other direction,* you're screwed.

Fang and I are wicked strong, and our wings are, uh, not superhuman—I guess super-avian would be the term. But these were some freaking stiff winds, and on top of that, it was, to put it in words that won't get edited out for younger kids, exceedingly cold.

Fang and I broke through the wind as best we could. We tried going above it, but before we got high enough, we realized we were so far up that we couldn't see squat on the ground, even with raptor vision.

Teeth clenched, windburn tears streaming out of our eyes, we headed back down, staying close to each other. We started in small circles, then made them increasingly larger. And saw nothing. Nothing but whiteness. Ice. Rock. Snow. Right then, global warming seemed like a great idea.

'Hypothermia,' Fang yelled over the wind, and I nodded, biting my lip. Dealing with regular old freezingness was one thing, but being caught somewhere, unable to move and keep warm, was something else. If Angel had fallen through some ice or had gotten trapped somehow, it wouldn't take long for her to freeze to death. Total, being smaller, would last even less time.

We kept seeing more of nothing. I realized that the wind was probably scouring away any tracks as fast as they could be made. I was so, so glad that Fang was with me, that we were doing this together. I looked over at him, his face focused and intent, and I felt a pang of— what? I didn't know. Sort of longing mixed with miserableness.

Feeling my eyes on him, he looked over at me, and his gaze seemed to go right inside my head, like a laser. I felt as if he could see right into my heart, see all my emotions, and I didn't know what to do. His expression softened, and he looked a bit surprised, but then he gave me his lopsided smile, and suddenly I was less miserable.

'We'll find her,' he called. 'We always do.'

I nodded, and our moment was gone.

It seemed as if we'd been flying forever, though it had probably been about fifteen minutes. But the coldness, the battling with the wind, the worry about Angel—it felt like a week since I'd decked Brian.

Then . . . I blinked several times and peered downward. Was that . . . ?

'There!' I said, pointing. 'Are those tracks?' Below us, I thought I saw faint gray outlines of very small tracks.

'Penguins?' Fang guessed. The prints were being scoured away by the wind even as we watched. I glanced ahead at where they were going, and sure enough, about a half mile away, I saw a huddled black-and-white blob of penguins grouped together to stay warm.

'Yeah,' I said, disappointment burning in my chest.

Then I thought: *penguins.*

'Penguins!' I shouted at Fang. He heard me, despite my voice being ripped away by the wind. My eyes felt frozen open, and my mouth was incredibly dry.

'That's what I just said!' he yelled back. Though he was only eight feet above me, I could hardly hear him.

'No, I mean, Angel wanted a penguin!' I shouted through cupped hands. 'I'm going down!' Fang nodded, and we angled downward, seeing the ground rushing up at us.

Please, please let Angel somehow be in the middle of the penguin huddle, keeping warm.

CHAPTER FIFTY-FOUR

The loss of his main contact was a regrettable obstacle, Gozen thought, but at least she had succeeded in placing tiny homing devices on the quarry before she was so unexpectedly terminated. Now Gozen watched his small screen as the green beacons began moving across the ice. He and his troops had been about to set out to find the beacon that had suddenly stopped and become dimmer, but then others had appeared, meaning more of his quarry had left the station. He'd wait till they stopped, then go out to meet them.

Head tilted on his gargantuan shoulders, Gozen listened to the wind. The storm was intensifying. Fortunately, neither he nor his troops would be much affected by it. It could even play into their plans.

He turned to his troops. 'Prepare for combat.'

CHAPTER FIFTY-FIVE

No, finding Angel huddled inside a warm mass of penguins would be too easy.

The second we landed, Fang and I were almost knocked off our feet. I quickly pulled in my wings and leaned into the wind. My face felt like it was being sanded with tiny ice crystals, and my cheeks were already burning.

Still, I tried to keep my eyes pried open enough to see the last traces of penguin tracks. Dropping to my knees, I looked carefully. Were those boot marks amid all the faint penguin footprints? There were no dog prints as far as I could tell. Any sign at all was being obliterated. Still, it was the only thing we'd found. I'd follow the tracks to the clump of penguins and then—like, question them or something.

I motioned to Fang and he nodded, reading my mind as easily as he always did. Not in an Angel-really-reading-my-mind kind of way, but in a Fang-knew-me-too-well kind of way. He stumbled slightly getting up, and I grabbed his hand and held it as we made our way toward the penguins.

Together we staggered forward, leaning into the wind, trying to keep on the trail between us and the penguins. Regular kids wouldn't have made it—they would have had to lie down to keep from being blown away. It was getting harder and harder to see, but the flock has a built-in navigator system that allows us to find our way places, even in the dark, even across huge distances.

It seemed like we'd been searching for hours. I was freezing, trembling with the cold, and really starting to panic. I was just beginning to think we'd never get there when with no warning, the ground gave way beneath my right foot. I yelped and stumbled, and Fang instinctively tightened his grip on my hand, hauling me up and back.

'Help!'

'Angel!' I screamed back, not knowing where her voice was coming from. I looked around blindly but could see nothing that would hide even a small bird kid.

'Max! Help!'

'We're here! We'll get you!' Fang kept his

arms around my waist while I cupped both hands around my mouth, shouting into the wind. 'Where are you?'

'Down here!' came her little voice. 'You just kicked snow on me!'

With that, Fang and I both dropped cautiously to our stomachs and inched forward until we saw the deep hole my foot had gone into. I brushed away some snow, and the hole got much bigger, fast.

'You're dumping snow on us!' Angel cried.

'I'm sorry!' I called. 'I have to find you first! We can't even see where you went in!'

Finally we brushed away enough snow to see the deep, deep crack in the ice, maybe a yard across at the surface, then plunging steeply down in an ever-narrowing vee. It was way too narrow for her to fly out, or for us to fly in. I remembered my flip reply to Brigid, that I would just fly out of a crevasse, and saw immediately that none of us could have flown out of there. No room.

'Get the rope,' I told Fang, but he was already uncoiling it. 'Angel? We're going to drop a rope down to you. Just hold on tight and we'll pull you up, okay?'

'Uh . . . ,' Angel said, her voice weak and tired.

'What?' Fang asked.

'My foot's stuck,' she said, sounding scared. 'And I have Total and Akila with me. They can't hold on to a rope.'

CHAPTER FIFTY-SIX

Normally I would have been swearing bitterly to myself at this point, but what with the Angel-reading-minds thing, I tried to hold off.

I looked over at Fang, lying next to me on the hard-packed snow. The strong wind was filling our mouths, noses, ears, and eyes with icy grit. 'Great,' I muttered, and he nodded.

'I'm sorry,' Angel called up, close to tears.

'It's okay,' I said. Years of successful lying stood me in good stead, and I sounded convincing even to me. 'Just hold tight for a second. . . .' *Plan, plan, need a plan.*

'It's awfully cold,' said Angel, teeth chattering. 'Akila and Total went to sleep, and they won't wake up.'

Oh, crap, I thought.

'Angel?' I called. 'The only way we can get the dogs out is if you tie the rope around them and we haul them out first. Then we'll get you.'

'Them first?' said Angel.

'They can't hold on to the rope, like you said. But you would have to be last. Or'—I had to give her all options—'or we can get you out first, if you really can't wait.'

172

Which meant leaving the dogs to die, if they weren't already dead. Silence, while Angel considered.

'I'll tie the rope around Total first,' Angel called up, and my heart flooded with pride.

Total was pretty light, so he was easy to pull up. When we got him out into the biting wind, he blinked and stirred a bit. Fang quickly zipped him inside his jacket. Fang himself was shaking with cold, and I knew having a big icicle next to him wouldn't help. We threw the rope down again and waited for eons while Angel tried to tie it around the much bigger dog.

'Akila's really heavy,' Angel finally called. 'I tied it on the best I could.'

Fang and I both pulled together, and we hauled up the eighty-pound dog without too much difficulty. As it had with Total, the frigid wind seemed to wake Akila up a bit when she got to the surface. I started rubbing her fur roughly all over, trying to get her blood going, while Fang dropped the rope into the crevasse again.

Total's voice came sleepily out of Fang's jacket. 'Angel? Akila?'

'They're okay,' Fang told him.

'Angel?' I called. 'They're both out. You did so good, sweetie! I'm so proud of you. Now you just hang on tight to the rope, okay? We'll have you up in a sec.'

'I got the rope,' Angel said, close to tears. 'But my foot's still stuck. I don't think I can get out.'

I looked at Fang in anguish. All of us were risking hypothermia. I already felt sleepy and weirdly warm, and Angel's voice was weaker and weaker. Plus, even if we got Angel out, would she be able to fly? How would we carry Akila? She weighed almost as much as I did.

Crap.

CHAPTER FIFTY-SEVEN

First things first, I thought.

'Angel, instead of holding on to the rope, tie it around your chest, under your arms. We'll pull you out.'

'But my—'

'I know, punkin,' I said determinedly. 'We'll just have to try.'

Fang and I together were strong enough to pull so hard that we'd break Angel's ankle. She wouldn't be able to hold on through that. Hence the tying. But at least she would be free. I still had no idea how to get Akila home.

'Okay, I'm ready,' came Angel's small voice.

Fang and I nodded to each other, then slowly, firmly pulled on the rope. There was hardly any give. I heard Angel make a little wail of pain, but we kept pulling as it became harder and harder. Suddenly Angel cried out, and the rope was much easier to pull.

'Angel?'

'My foot's out,' she said miserably.

We had her up top in a few seconds, and then we were both hugging her.

Angel looked up at me, her face shockingly white. 'We won't make it back,' she said. 'Not in this storm.'

'She's right,' Fang said. 'We need to dig a hole and hunker down, wait it out.'

It took me only a second to agree. Carefully we stepped away from the crevasse and began looking for shelter. There was a rocky outcropping about ten yards away, and slowly, painfully, we dragged ourselves there, holding tightly to Angel and Akila.

Angel and the dogs crouched down while Fang and I dug out a cave as fast as we could. Since our hands were frozen and we couldn't feel them, this took longer than we hoped. Finally it was big enough to hold all of us— barely. We grabbed Angel, Total, and Akila, and pulled them into our makeshift shelter. Fang and I kept our backs to the wind, and within a minute, the storm had blown enough snow to seal us in. It was amazing how the wall deadened the sound outside. The lack of wind howling in my ears was deafening.

I took off my sunglasses and checked us all

out. Angel was still pale and shaking with cold. Fang was trying hard not to shiver, but he was obviously grimly miserable. Total was struggling to his feet. Akila was standing uncertainly, pressed against the back wall of the shelter. Her thick fur was full of ice, and I quickly rubbed my gloved hands over her, brushing the ice to the ground.

'How's your ankle, Angel?' I asked.

'It hurts. It might not be actually broken, though. Don't know. It hurts.' She was wiped, hardly able to speak.

'Okay, everyone, rub your arms and slap your hands against your chest,' I ordered, fighting the urge to just lie down and go to sleep. It was quiet in here, cozy almost, and maybe I was imagining it, but I felt warmer. 'Get that blood going!' I reached over and rubbed Total's fur. 'How you doin'?'

'I'd give a lot for one of those thermal pools about now,' he said, his voice thin and crackly.

'You and me both,' I said with feeling. I glanced at Fang. 'Too bad Brigid isn't here. I bet she'd know what to do.' I probably only sounded about 70 percent bitter.

Fang met my gaze evenly. 'I'm sure she'll come find our frozen bodies.'

'We're not gonna freeze!' Angel said anxiously. 'Are we?'

Instantly I regretted baiting Fang, but what do you know, even a little bit of anger warms you right up. 'No, sweetie, we have this shelter. We'll be okay,' I said. 'We'll just wait out the storm, and as soon as it's over, we'll all get back to the station.'

I wondered if the others had got caught in the storm. I sure hoped not. I was totally not up for rescuing anyone else.

CHAPTER FIFTY-EIGHT

Here's a tip: If you're ever stuck in an ice cave in the middle of a storm with two bird kids, a talking dog, and another dog, do yourself a favor: Bring a book. 'Cause once it seems as though you might not die any second, it suddenly becomes intensely boring. And if Total hummed another song from *My Fair Lady*, I was gonna throw him back out into the blizzard.

'I'm cold,' said Angel, then caught herself, sitting up straight. 'Not that cold.'

That was my brave little soldier. Tough as nails.

'And my ankle's so cold it doesn't hurt much,' she said with a little smile.

We had to get her back to the station, have someone look at her ankle. We all heal supernaturally fast, but if her ankle was broken and it healed wrong, they'd have to rebreak it.

The storm was still howling outside, as far as we could tell. I was starting to feel sleepy again—one of the early warning signs of hypothermia. This space was too small for us to move around to keep warm, and despite the fact that we were packed in like sardines, we didn't seem to be warming one another up. It was slowly growing darker and darker as the storm made our snow wall thicker.

I tried thinking angry thoughts to get my blood warm, but after just a few minutes it seemed like too much trouble.

'This is the end,' Total said.

'What?' I said. 'No, it's not. This is not the end.' I wanted to say a bunch more, but it seemed so hard to speak. 'It's not the end till I say it's the end.' My tongue felt thick, my mouth dry. Brigid had told us not to eat snow for water, but I was dying to.

'This is one thing you can't control, Max,' said Fang. Angel was leaning sleepily against him, and he was stroking her hair.

Well, I just didn't accept that.

'It's been an honor serving with you,' Total intoned mournfully. I started to break in, but he held up a paw. 'No, no, don't stop me. Certain things must be said. I always swore I'd face death with dignity and honor.'

'No, you didn't!' I exclaimed. 'You always said you'd fight it tooth and nail! You said you'd go out kicking and screaming!'

Total frowned at me, then went on as if I hadn't spoken.

'Life, like that first burst of color at dawn, is fleeting,' he said. 'Ah, sweet life! What a short, strange trip it's been! I've done, *been*, so much more than a typical dog.' He looked fondly at Akila. 'Just like you, my beauty, my queen. You've served a nobler purpose.'

I found I had enough energy to roll my eyes.

'And now it's come to this.' Total gestured to our tiny, ever-darker cave. 'I had such dreams, such hopes! There's a whole world out there. . . .' He shook his head. 'I always wanted to be an astronaut. Now I'll never even get to try my wings.' In the dim light, I saw his tiny baby wings flutter slightly, and for some reason, I got a lump in my throat.

I blamed it on the hypothermia and near death.

'How many fine wines I haven't tried.' Total sighed. 'How many sights I haven't seen. The Pyramids in Egypt. The Great Wall of China. The bonny, bonny White Cliffs of Dover. Gone, all gone, lost to me forever!'

'Please tell me the end is soon,' Fang muttered.

Suddenly I had a thought: air. We were sealed into this place. Had we used up all the oxygen? Was that why we were so dopey? I twisted around and punched my fist through the snow wall as hard as I could. My hand was so numb it was like I was using a stick. A gust of fresh, icy air blew in, and we all inhaled and blinked.

'Is the storm over?' Angel mumbled.

'No,' came a deep, odd voice from outside.

My eyes flew open wide, and so did Fang's. Normally my body would have been instantly flooded with adrenaline and I'd have been in full-on fight mode, but this time I could barely react, barely raise my arm.

'The storm is just beginning.' The deep voice laughed, and then the wall crashed down on us.

CHAPTER FIFTY-NINE

They were ghosts, ice ghosts, my brain thought sluggishly.

Except ghosts couldn't drag us out into the freezing air. Despite being half dead from hypothermia, Fang and I still had enough strength to immediately throw ourselves into the air, each of us holding one of Angel's hands.

'Agh!' I cried, feeling a fine wire net smash against my face. The net whipped us down against the icy ground hard enough to make me lose my breath.

'Max!' Angel cried.

Pushing myself up on my numb hands, I searched frantically for a way out, at the same time trying to identify our attackers. The storm had lessened a bit, so I could see at least a couple feet in front of me. I blinked up through the mesh and saw that our captors were some kind of jazzed-up robots, kind of like short Flyboys with no wings. Only they hadn't bothered making them look even halfway human.

We just couldn't get a break.

Fury warmed my blood, and I tried to leap up, snarling, but the net only closed tighter around us, knocking me to the ground again.

I heard laughter, and spun my head this way and that to identify its source. The wind still howled in my ears, making it hard to tell where the laughter had come from.

One of the things was bigger than the others, who were only four feet tall or so.

'Do not hurt them,' he said in the deep, gravelly voice we'd first heard. 'Remember, we must save them.'

'News flash,' I spat, trying to rise up again. 'Your saving us is practically killing us! Let us up!'

He laughed again, but his face didn't change expression, which was way creepy. I squinted, trying to get a better view. 'Oh, jeez,' I muttered in disgust. Clearly they had gotten this guy from Frank-n-steins R Us. First off, he was enormous—maybe seven feet tall. And huge, broad and heavy. One arm was like an I beam: way too long, out of proportion with the rest of his body. I could barely make out metal spikes that seemed embedded in his flesh. Gross. He gave an impression of being chunked together from different alien species, and somehow it seemed even worse than Ari's awful wings, sewn into his back.

'Not saving you from this storm, mutant,' he said. 'Saving you for your later fate, we are.'

His voice was weirdly inflected and metallic, like an automated answering machine.

'Oh, good. Yoda captured us,' Fang whispered.

Something hauled the net up with us in it, and we dangled a foot off the ground. Fang was hyped, also trying hard to get out. Angel still looked shocky and frozen, confused and scared. Total was struggling to right himself, and Akila couldn't get on her feet, but she was growling.

'I am Gozen,' said the bigger thing. 'I do not want you to freeze to death. I want to watch you die later.'

'You need to get yourself a new hobby,' I snarled.

'It's always *some*thing,' Total muttered, still trying to get upright.

'Killing things is not a hobby,' Gozen said, sounding as though he would have smiled if he could. 'It is my life. It is what I was created to do. I am able to kill things in many, many different ways.'

Gross, I thought. Someone had programmed him to feel pleasure about killing. I could hear it in his voice.

'We're able to kill things in many different ways too,' I said, putting as much steel into my voice as I could, in case he was programmed to pick up on stuff like that. 'We like breaking things, for instance.' I shifted my glance to one of the robot soldiers, deciding that if we all suddenly swung toward it, we could move the net enough for me to try to kick its head off.

'That is something we share,' said Gozen. His clawlike hand shot out before I could blink, and he grabbed Angel's arm through the net. 'Like this.'

We all heard the horrible, unmistakable sound of Angel's bone snapping, accompanied by her barely suppressed shriek of pain. My heart leaped into my throat, and I chopped down on Gozen's hand as best I could. My hand bounced off his grip, and the rebound almost dislocated my shoulder. *Way to go, Max. Chop down on solid metal.*

Gozen released Angel, and I immediately grabbed her, drawing her to me and holding her against my chest, feeling her trying to stifle her cries. We were still swinging above the ground, and the mesh wasn't stopping the

183

freezing winds from tearing at our faces, our jackets.

'Move them,' Gozen directed.

Whatever was holding us started moving slowly across the ice. I felt as if I'd been cold forever, had been surrounded by screaming wind my whole life. Inside the swinging mesh, I looked at Fang's eyes, the only dark things visible in the endless, swirling whiteness.

Wait, he seemed to say. *Wait, and when we see a chance, we'll take it.*

Part Three

MOON OVER MIAMI—OR SOMETHING LIKE THAT

CHAPTER SIXTY

Holding us off the ground inside a tightly woven metal net was about as effective as locking us in dog crates. Not infallible, but pretty dang close. Sure, we could move the net by shifting our weight around, but we were too far away from anything to hit.

After a while we stopped shivering and got sleepy again—welcome back, hypothermia! Just as I was groggily debating the merits of freezing to death before anyone could do something awful to us versus actually living, the thing carrying us began to roll up a snow-covered ramp. My eyes were burning, and my lashes were frozen with chunks of ice, but I blinked and squinted. We were going into . . . a building? A large, round, white building?

Inside I saw that it was a really big jet, designed to move troops or cars or something. So we were going somewhere.

'Max?' That voice . . .

The net released us, hard, onto the floor. Angel gasped slightly, but fortunately she was so out of it by now that the new pain barely registered.

In an instant I staggered to my feet, willing myself back to full consciousness. The ramp closed, and my eyes couldn't see well in the dim light. I'd lost my sunglasses in the skirmish and was now practically snow-blind.

'Max!'

My heart sank, and I peered into the half-light. 'Gazzy?'

CHAPTER SIXTY-ONE

Half an hour later, we were thawed, reunited with the rest of the flock, able to see, and becoming very, very p.o.'d about being captives *again*. Yeah, pretty much business as usual for us.

'Where are we going?' Iggy asked. 'Any clues?'

'No,' I said. This rear area of the plane, intended for cargo, had not been graced with windows, since *boxes* usually don't give a crap about where they're going. We were lucky it was slightly heated.

'Who was the big thug?' Nudge wrapped her arms around her knees, resting her head on them. They'd been grabbed one by one, back at the station. Some of the scientists had tried to fight and had a bunch of serious injuries to show for it. I felt sorry for them, but if you lie down with dogs . . . (No, Total, don't get offended. The flock were the 'dogs' in that metaphor. See, they hung out with— You

188

know what? To heck with it.)

'Don't know,' I said. Adrenaline had been keeping me alert when we first got here, but now it was gone, leaving me wallowing in the wallow of the deeply bummed. 'He's a big Frankenberry jerk, though.'

'Those things are so weird,' said Gazzy.

'You're not kidding,' I agreed.

All the short soldiers that had captured us, plus a bunch more, were here in the cargo area with us. When the ramp had locked into place, the big guy had given a command. The soldiers had lined up against the wall, three rows deep, and then just stood there. I couldn't tell if they were powered down or what.

Then Gazzy had tried to touch one and got a nasty electric shock that knocked him backward about a foot and a half.

Several of the soldiers around that one had seemed to power up then, shifting their positions and aiming their sensors at us. A couple of them had inched forward, and we all froze.

'Back away very slowly, Gazzy,' I said quietly. 'To the wall, and sit down, very, very slowly.'

Still rubbing his shocked hand, Gazzy began to back up, then he jumped when a laser beam shot out and burned a hole right through the toe of his boot.

'Yow!' he said, hopping on the other foot.

189

'Did it get you?' I asked anxiously, keeping my eyes on the soldiers.

'No—just burned a hole through my boot. Missed my toes.'

'Okay, everyone, let's just stay still,' I ordered. 'No sudden moves. These things are clearly hair-trigger, and I don't want any holes burned through more important stuff, like our heads.'

Fifteen minutes later, we were all ready to be diagnosed with ADD, and the sitting-still thing was not working for us. Gradually we found out that we could move, as long as we didn't do anything suddenly and didn't go near the soldiers.

'Fine, they can have me if they want, but why drag Akila into this?' Total said for the nineteenth time. 'She didn't do anything!'

'I'm sorry,' I said, trying for the nineteenth time not to choke him to death. 'On the other hand, if they'd left her, she might be dead by now.'

'Hmph!' Total said. Akila, I was glad to see, was looking relatively undamaged—though haughty, as if all this being captured was okay for ordinary mutants, but not for a purebred Malamute whose mother had once won the Iditarod dog sled race.

But I was relieved she seemed all right. I might feel murderous toward any number of enemies, but I always had a soft spot in my

190

heart for animals. Especially non-genetically engineered ones.

I inched over to sit next to Fang, and had to look around, startled, for a couple moments before I saw him, almost invisible against the dark wall. I wondered if he was missing Dr. Amazing, then felt bad for still being jealous of her. Nudge had told me how hard Brigid and the others had fought against the GoBots.

I was glad Angel was finally sleeping, her head in Fang's lap. We'd made her a lame sling out of a scarf, but I hoped someone would set her arm soon. Someone like my mom.

The metal door at the front of the cargo area opened, and the big thug came back in. His footsteps made him sound like he weighed about three hundred pounds, and now I could gauge his height at almost seven feet.

I allowed myself a quick fantasy of making him swallow one of Gazzy's bombs, then forced myself to full-alert mode, looking for a way out of this mess. As soon as we'd been locked in, we'd tried unsuccessfully to open the back ramp—everything would have been sucked out of the plane if we'd opened it, which was fine for us, since we could fly. The minibots would all have gone crunch on the ground, of course, but hey, you win some, you lose some.

'Who are you?' Nudge asked bravely.

'I am Gozen,' the big thing said.

Nudge's brow wrinkled. 'Like Japanese dumplings?'

CHAPTER SIXTY-TWO

'That would be *gyoza*,' Fang murmured at Nudge.

'Where do you come from, Gozen?' I said, feeling fresh rage wash over me at what he'd done to Angel. 'Whose henchman are you?'

Gozen turned his big head to look down at me—looked down with his nonhuman eyes that glowed blue. 'I am Gozen. I am the leader. You will be quiet.'

'Good luck with that,' I heard Iggy mutter.

'We will be landing in fourteen hours, thirty-nine minutes,' said Gozen.

Okay, what was fifteen hours away from Antarctica? Well, actually, most of the world. Not Canada or northern Europe, not the Arctic. But we could be headed most other places. Good thing I had narrowed that down.

'Where are we going?' I tried.

'That is not your concern.'

'Au contraire, Your Trollness,' I said, standing up. 'We're very concerned. We have *appointments*. Places to go, people to see. Now tell us where the hell we're going!'

Faster than my eyes (with raptor vision)

192

could track, one thick leg shot out and whipped my feet out from under me. I caught myself on my hands just in time for him to kick my side hard enough to make my breath fly out of my lungs and give me that so-attractive fish-gasping expression.

The flock, except for Angel, was on their feet in a second, but I made a 'Don't attack' gesture—just in time, because the soldiers had once again shifted forward. With iron control, I slowly sucked in my breath, hoping they wouldn't start lasering everything in sight. I took inventory: legs okay; ribs really, really bruised, maybe cracked. It hurt a surprising amount, which made me realize that it had been a while since I'd had broken bones. Clearly I needed to review my street-fighting skills.

'You do not give orders,' Gozen said in his weird almost-human-but-not-quite voice. 'You follow orders.'

I bit my lip so I wouldn't tell him to go stuff his orders. Apparently he picked up on things like that. Gozen was unlike anything we'd come up against before. He was bigger, faster, human enough to be subtle but machine enough to have no conscience. I did think he was probably too heavy to fly, so yay for that.

I gathered my feet under me, refusing to wince. Keeping a sharp eye on Gozen, I stood up cautiously, motioning the others behind my

193

back to stay out of his range. Unless he could shoot bullets from his eyes, which I wasn't putting past him.

'We are against global warming,' Gozen intoned.

Was that a statement or a question? Were we part of the 'we'?

'Uh-huh,' I said carefully, backing away slowly. 'That's good.'

'Therefore we are violently opposed to your kind,' Gozen went on.

Not so good.

I quickly decided I believed in global warming. 'But we're against it too!' I said, keeping one wary eye on the Transformer-bots. 'We were in Antarctica helping to stop global warming!'

'No. Humans created the problem. Humans are destroying the earth. You are destroying life.'

'Okay, now, see, you're wrong here on a bunch of levels,' I said quickly. 'First, we're not even completely human! Did you miss the wings? I mean, jeez. Plus, as I just pointed out, we were trying to stop global warming! We're totally against it!'

'Yeah!' said Gazzy. 'We're trying to save the world! It's our mission!'

Gozen turned slowly, and my heart sped up when his gaze stopped on Gazzy. I moved to put myself between them.

'You are part of the problem,' Gozen said with a machine's horrible, inflexible logic that always turns out to be wrong because there's something crucial missing from the formula. 'I will enjoy your death.' With that, he turned and exited through the door at the front of the cargo area. I wished one of us—okay, me—had thought of trying to escape through that door while Gozen wasn't looking.

Once the door was shut behind him and we heard the ominous click of the lock, Fang said, 'That guy has no sense of humor.'

'No,' I agreed, sitting down gingerly to avoid hurting my ribs even more. 'And I've thought of something else, much worse.'

'What?' asked Nudge.

'We have fourteen hours to go,' I said. 'And I doubt we're getting meal service or in-flight entertainment.'

CHAPTER SIXTY-THREE

Okay, so they kidnapped us from Antarctica. Let's review: extremely freezing, much ice, snow, wind, et cetera. Very little fresh fruit. No swimsuit season. No cable TV. No coffee shops.

Where did they bring us *to?*

Miami.

You'd think it would work the other way—snatched *away* from Miami, sent *to* Antarctica, which is like Siberia but with more penguins.

But no.

Just another example of the whimsy of the fantastically wealthy, powerful, and deluded. For us, it was like, Oh, please don't snatch us away from Antarctica and send us to the playground of the rich and famous! Not that briar patch!

On the other hand: In Antarctica we were relatively free and doing actual meaningful work that we felt good about. In Miami we were prisoners. It was an ironic situation all around, no doubt about it.

I won't bore you with the usual duct-taped hands and feet, bound wings, stuck into black body bags, yada yada yada, that we always go through in these ho-hum random abductions. It was like, same old, same old, and I could hardly work up the energy to fight hard enough to get more than a black eye and a sprained wrist out of it.

I guess I'm just getting jaded.

When they unzipped our bags and started ripping off the tape (tip: Don't try that at home), we found we were high up in a tall, tall building. There were tons of other tall buildings around us. Below us was one of Florida's white-sugar beaches, edged by water that I was dying to sink into. Or at least I'd want to after it stopped pouring. The sky was full of dark gray clouds. It was raining so hard I could hear the drops pelting the window glass like BBs.

I was amazed they had let us loose in a room with windows, given our annoying habit of leaping through them, but ole Gozen answered that question.

'These windows have been rated for hurricane-force winds of up to one hundred twenty miles per hour,' he intoned. 'They do not open from the inside.' He stepped closer, then heaved himself sideways, shoulder first, into one of the big plate glass windows. We all winced, expecting him to go bye-bye with a huge crash, but instead he practically bounced off, the glass not even cracking, and I thought, *Holy crap.* Or, actually, much worse than holy crap, but let's just say I thought holy crap.

'The auction will begin in one hour,' Gozen said. 'Food will be provided.'

'You know, he's really a people person,' I said when he'd left.

'What auction was he talking about?' Gazzy asked, and I shrugged.

'No clue,' I answered, starting to walk around. The double doors to the room were metal, windowless, and had several locking bolts. Our captors definitely thought we were hot stuff, and I felt kind of proud of our bad reputation. Proud but really trapped.

'Now what?' Angel was still wan and pale, with dark circles under her eyes. There were chairs around a table, and I helped her sit in one.

'Iggy?' I said. He came closer, and with his incredibly delicate touch, he skimmed his fingers over her arm. 'Is there anything you can do?'

'It's really swollen,' he said, and I used every bit of my self-control to not say, 'No duh!'

'It feels like a clean break,' Iggy went on. 'Let me see . . . So to speak.' Very tenderly, he manipulated her broken arm.

Though Angel's face got a little green around the edges, she made hardly a sound. I held her shoulders and sent her comforting thoughts, and then we all heard a tiny scrape and a clicking sound, and Angel relaxed a bit.

'Oh, that feels better,' she said. 'Still really bad, but less bad. Thanks, Iggy.'

Iggy smiled, proud that he could contribute to the flock this way. I ripped up the lining of my jacket—wouldn't be needing that here!— and made a stiff bandage to hold her arm in place.

'Now what?' Gazzy repeated Angel's question.

'Fan out, check the perimeter,' I ordered.

Which took less than five minutes.

Everyone reported that the room seemed rock solid. The vents were too small for a house cat, there was only the one set of doors, and we had all seen the window demonstration.

'Maybe I can . . .' Nudge murmured, and she crouched next to one of the doors. She moved her fingers close to the locks and closed her eyes. 'If I could make the bolts all line up . . .'

'Oh, so smart, Nudge,' I breathed, coming to crouch next to her. 'Can you feel them?'

'I think so,' she said. 'If my magnetism could—ow!'

There was a harsh crackle, and Nudge was jolted backward almost a foot. The residual electricity practically made my hair stand on end. Nudge was on her back, rubbing her hands.

'The locks are booby-trapped,' she announced glumly, in case we hadn't picked up on it. 'So much for my new skill.'

'My new skill was no help either,' said Angel.

'And since we're not surrounded by snow, I'm still blind.' Iggy sounded bitter, but then he perked up. 'On the other hand, this carpet is a tasteful ecru, with a thin cinnamon stripe close to the wall.'

I glanced at Fang, who was totally visible against the walnut paneling of the room. He shrugged.

'So now I guess we wait,' I said. Which, you

know, I'm *so good* at.

CHAPTER SIXTY-FOUR

Being in this tall building was interesting for us, because we were up high but not flying. Outside, it was really storming—huge crashes of thunder and lightning that I remembered from the last time we were here in the wishfully named Sunshine State. Gusts of wind buffeted the building, and it was so tall it actually swayed.

'Good thing this building's rated for hurricane-force winds,' Nudge said, looking out the window nervously. 'It's really blowing out there.'

They fed us. I was hoping they'd send in actual humans with our food, because they're easy to jump and pretty fragile. No problem getting past them, unless they have guns.

Instead we got Transformer-bots with trays, under Gozen's watchful laser eyes.

They gave us a variety of food, apparently never having fed mutant bird kids before. We had oatmeal, sandwiches, fruit, bread, a bowl of dog kibble, which Total pushed toward Akila, and . . .

'Oh, my God!' Nudge squealed, removing the cover on a tray. 'Oh, my God!'

'What? What?' I hurried over, hoping for chocolate.

Instead I was confronted with a large bowl of . . . well, birdseed.

'It's just seeds!' Nudge said. 'Not even like a granola bar. It's *birdseed!*'

For a couple seconds we all just stared at one another, and then we cracked up, really howling with laughter.

'Oh, God, no!' I said, holding my bruised ribs. 'Don't make me laugh!'

'Nummy!' Gazzy said, poking the seeds with his finger. 'Could I get some worms with this?'

'Stop! Stop!' I begged.

Even Fang, who as you know is Mr. Personality, was actually laughing out loud, bent over, his hands on his knees.

'What? Seeds?' Iggy asked, feeling the contents of the bowl. 'Is this really birdseed? 'Cause we're *birds?*'

I nodded, tears running down my cheeks. I gasped for air, saying 'Ouch' with each breath. 'I'm nodding, Ig.'

'This is too much,' Fang wheezed. 'Too much! Birdseed! Oh, God.'

'What's for dessert? *Caterpillars?*' I said, barely intelligibly. This set off a new round of shrieking laughter.

'This sandwich isn't half bad,' Total said, his paws up on the table.

'Did they bring us a bunch of nesting

201

material?' Gazzy asked. ' 'Cause I'm beat.'

More laughter. Angel almost fell onto her hurt arm.

The door opened, and we tried to whip ourselves into fighting form but failed miserably. This was one way they'd never tried to subdue us—with laughter. Akila immediately got to her feet, ears back, head lowered. She looked pretty scary, but all I could do was try to swallow my giggles.

Gozen stood in the doorway, watching us with his glowing blue eyes. 'You will not find the rest of the day amusing,' he said. 'Follow me. The auction is about to begin. As is the hurricane.'

Fang and I looked at each other with 'huh?' faces. *What hurricane?*

'Question,' I said, raising a finger. 'What auction are we talking about? And did you just say *hurricane?*'

Gozen had turned toward the door, and now he turned back. 'The Uber-Director is auctioning you off to the highest bidder. He expects you to bring a great deal of money.'

'I'm flattered,' I said. 'What are we being sold for?'

'Whatever they want.'

Okay, that wouldn't end well.

'And the hurricane?' I asked. Wasn't the end of hurricane season, like, November? How could there be a hurricane now?

'There is a Category four hurricane about to make a direct hit on Miami,' Gozen intoned. I wondered if worry had been programmed into him, and decided probably not. It would just get in the way.

'Uh-huh,' I said. 'Does anyone seem, um, concerned about that? Category four is one of the big ones, right?'

'The city has been evacuated,' Gozen told us.

'But not us?'

'No.' He opened the door and gestured to it.

Fang went first, the others falling into line behind him, me bringing up the rear. I was almost out the door when my gaze fell on the bowl of freaking *birdseed,* and I cracked up all over again.

CHAPTER SIXTY-FIVE

Considering I'm not the world's youngest executive, I sure have been in a lot of corporate conference rooms. They're all pretty much the same: big plate glass windows; huge table, usually rectangular or oblong; large potted plants; thick carpet; rolley chairs.

This one had a wall of flat TV screens, and something that I'd never seen before: a transparent *person,* with his organs and stuff in clear Plexiglas boxes, and his head attached to one by an almost-bare spinal cord. He was sitting—or stacked, more accurately—in a customized wheelchair.

He saw all of us staring at him, and wheeled silently over the carpet toward us.

'I am the Uber-Director,' he said, his voice a lot like Gozen's: with human but slightly odd inflections, and also a barely detectable mechanical quality. Looking closer, I saw that his guts and stuff were surrounded by and connected to machine parts—hoses, pumps, electronic things. And yes, it was *totally* as gross as it sounds. If I hadn't already seen a million incredibly gross things in my life, I would have barfed right there.

His voice had enough expression to convince me that he had a colossal ego jam-packed into his Habitrail body. Great. I *thought* this day had been a little lacking in megalomaniacs.

None of us said anything—no leaping forward with outstretched hands and big smiles. I guess we just weren't raised right.

'I've been concerned with you for quite some time,' he went on.

'That makes . . . almost one of us,' I said.

Unlike Gozen, the UD could smile. Or frown. 'I find you very . . . interesting. From a scientific viewpoint, of course.'

'Uh-huh,' I said, staring at him in

fascination. 'I have a bit of scientific curiosity myself. Listen, how do they keep your boxes clean? Like, with an aquarium vacuum, or what?'

The Uber-Director had been gifted with the blush response to anger, and now his waxy cheeks mottled with a yucky purple color that would put me off plum pudding for the rest of my life.

He glared at Gozen. Gozen took several quick steps toward me, raising his oversize arm. I leaped onto the table, wings out, ready to fly around like a bat out of hell just to freak them out. Outside, strong winds pummeled the windows, and heavy rain all but obliterated from view the tall buildings around us. The thunder and lightning were constant. Yep, looked like a hurricane, all right.

Gozen froze.

I looked down at the Uber-Director. He was staring at me with a mixture of outrage . . . and hunger.

'Uh, you okay, UD?' I asked. 'Is it okay if I call you UD?' I looked at Gozen. 'Is he okay? Does he need a feed bag hooked up or something?'

Gozen lunged for me, but I jumped backward. His powerful fist, the size of a ham, crashed down on the table, bouncing me slightly. The table splintered, and I skittered to the other end. I knew my flock was on alert, and I took a second to glance at BoxBoy. His head was leaning to one side, as if he was tired, and I got the impression that if he had hands, he would have been rubbing his brow.

'Enough, Gozen,' he said softly, and just like that, Gozen straightened and backed up until he stood stiffly against one wall. If only I could get Gazzy and Iggy to obey orders like that.

'Get off the table,' the UD said to me. 'The auction is about to begin. Once the monitors are on, you will all be silent.'

I heard Gazzy stifle a laugh.

The UD's eyes met mine. 'Do you have anything to say before the monitors are activated?'

'Yes.' I kept a straight face. 'A hamster called. He wants his home back.'

CHAPTER SIXTY-SIX

I had to hand it to whoever was running things: They'd learned to take regular humans out of the equation. We'd always beaten them, confused them, gotten through them somehow. Which was why we were left with BoxBoy, the Incredible Humorless Hulk, and a bunch of Transformer-bots.

With a slight electronic crackle, the wall of TV screens came to life. One by one, their screen snow was replaced by a person. There were both men and women, in all kinds of settings. The one thing they had in common was that they all oozed power like radiation. Clearly they were looking at screens of their own—I saw their eyes dart around, linger for just a second on the UD with a hint of distaste, then fasten on us.

I looked at the UD. 'What, eBay isn't good enough for us?'

If anyone had been familiar with the evil smile on Iggy's face, they would have questioned the decision to put us on camera. But oh well. Live and learn, is what I say.

'Here are the objects available for auction.' The UD's voice was surprisingly strong and commanding. 'They are in decent shape, though one is damaged.'

That would be Angel's broken arm. I got mad all over again.

'Do they have any . . . liabilities?' A woman with dark hair and eyes, wearing a severe navy suit, spoke first.

'Besides our woeful fashion sense?' I asked before the UD could respond.

Every face on the screens looked surprised. No one was expecting us to talk.

'Our lack of commitment to personal hygiene?'

'You will be silent!' the UD hissed at me. But since Gozen stayed where he was, I didn't take him seriously.

I raised my eyebrows, looking directly at the faces on the screens. 'I guess it depends on whether you consider a complete inability to follow orders a *liability.*'

'Silence!' the UD said again as the people on the screens began to murmur to their unseen partners. He spoke to them: 'As you can see, they are functional, with a limited, though useful, intelligence.'

'Limited intelligence?' I broke in, outraged. 'Bite me! You're kind of the last person to talk about *limitations!* At least I can . . . swim! And fly! And digest by myself!'

'Yeah, or how about this?' the Gasman said, and then he erupted . . . his new skill. I'd been wondering if he would develop one, and what form it would take. Maybe he'd be able to read minds, like Angel? Fly superfast, like me? Feel colors, like Iggy? It could have been anything.

But of course it wasn't.

I swear to you, it was literally a green mushroom cloud. I mean, he'd always had a messed-up digestive system. Gazzy in a small room with you meant you'd soon have tears in your eyes. And I guess most boys hone their ability to let rip on command to a fine, subtle art.

This was in a completely different league.

I saw eyes widen onscreen. The UD turned to see the flock moving rapidly away from

Gazzy, who looked as if he were being enveloped in, well, a cloud of noxious gas, colored a sulfurous yellow green. He was grinning. 'Ah, that's better. Better out than in!'

'Jesus, Mary, and Joseph,' Total said hoarsely, and ran under the conference table.

'Whoa!' I said, gagging. 'What have you been *eating*? Kryptonite? Nuclear waste?'

'What is that? Who did that? What does this mean?' Voices from the screens mingled together. The UD was looking at Gazzy with confusion and anger.

I pressed my hand over my mouth and nose and got as far from Gazzy as the room allowed. Close to the screens, I spoke through my hand, trying not to inhale.

'It really just depends on your definition of *liability*,' I said nasally.

'It's a new skill!' Gazzy announced, sounding excited.

'Good God,' Nudge muttered, pressing herself against the farthest wall. 'Why don't these windows *open*?'

'You are the *man!*' Iggy said, and he and Gazzy slapped high fives. It's a guy thing.

And that pretty much set the tone for the rest of the auction.

Iggy picked his nose. Fang blended into a dark painting that consisted of paint splatters and drips. Nudge kept up a constant chatter—at one point going on about different colors of nail polish and whether something with glitter was really appropriate for day wear—though you could hardly hear it over the rising wind.

Okay, call me alarmist, but it sounded incredibly bad out there, and a Category 4 hurricane with mandatory evacuation did not seem like a good scene. I'd flown in some pretty intense storms, but if we'd been outside now, we would have been splattered against the building like gnats.

Sure, these windows were superstrong, but all the same, the wind was a tad concerning. I motioned to the others to move toward the inside walls, away from the glass.

'Attention!' The UD's face was that awful blotchy purple color again. Ugh. 'Can we return to the business at hand? There's a bid on the table of half a billion dollars. Can I hear three-quarters of a billion?'

You know, half a billion dollars just doesn't go as far as it used to.

'One more thing,' I said to the screens, raising my voice to be heard. 'We all have expiration dates. If you buy us, you should know that it's a limited-time offer. We're probably single-use mutants, pretty much.'

'A single use might be all that's required of you,' the Uber-Director said silkily, then went back to the bidding.

And that was when the superstrong, hurricane-rated, Gozen-bounced-against fancy windows all imploded.

CHAPTER SIXTY-SEVEN

In case you don't know, safety glass can still shatter. They call it safety glass because it tends to shatter into somewhat-less-sharp cubes, rather than saberlike shards. Little bit of info for ya there. See? I'm fun *and* educational!

In the next second, we were all slammed against the back wall, as the wind blasted in through the broken windows, seeming as if it wanted to snatch us out into the storm.

'Gozen!' the UD screamed. I wondered if he had volume buttons for 'scream' or could just raise his voice. Anyway, Gozen heard him and lumbered awkwardly over to the wheelchair, putting himself between the window and the UD.

'Flock!' I bellowed. 'Get down! Under the table!'

Immediately Fang, Angel, Nudge, Iggy, Total, and Gazzy rolled under the table. I grabbed Akila's collar and dragged her under with me. Around us, chairs were whipping around, smashing against the walls, getting sucked out the windows.

'Can we fly out?' Gazzy asked, almost

shouting.

Fang and I both shook our heads. 'The wind is too strong. We should get out into the hallway,' Fang said, and I nodded.

Angel was watching something out in the room. The remote control for one of the big-screen TVs must have whizzed around and smacked up against something that caused it to flip channels.

'What is it, Ange?' I said.

'There's a hurricane report on TV,' she said. 'It says it's almost a Category five, and they think it was caused by global warming.'

There was that global warming again!

'There have always been hurricanes,' I pointed out.

'Not at this time of year. Plus, there are many, many more of them now, and they tend to be stronger and more destructive,' Fang told me.

I looked at him. 'Okay, maybe global warming is bad,' I admitted.

He made a no-freaking-duh face, and then said, 'Category fives have winds more than a hundred fifty-five miles an hour. In other words, enough to rip most things apart. Including us. There's no way we can fly in it.'

'Okay, hallway it is,' I said. 'We'll get out there and see if there's any place we can wait out the storm. Fang, you're in charge of Akila.'

'We are *not* leaving her!' Total stated.

'I know,' I said. 'Gazzy, Nudge, and Angel, stick as close to me as possible. Everyone ready?'

Five pairs of determined bird kid eyes met mine.

'Okay. Let's do this thing.'

CHAPTER SIXTY-EIGHT

Our plan was to roll out from under the table and crawl fast to the double doors, avoiding Gozen and the UD if at all possible. While I had been bantering with the buyers, Fang and Iggy had been very productive: They'd shredded a couple of our Antarctica coats and knotted them into several long lengths of rope. Now Fang tied one to Akila's collar, and Iggy tied one around Total's middle.

'It's not a leash!' I snapped as he protested. 'It's so we don't lose you!'

The electricity was off in the conference room now. The wall of TVs had been shattered. Lots of stuff had been sucked out the windows, and other things were hurtling around.

'Gozen!' the Uber-Director shouted. 'Don't let them escape!'

Gozen began to move toward us, his bulk and weight helping to keep him steady. The

UD's wheelchair was being knocked about, and if I were him, I would have been freaking out, waiting to break apart into messy building blocks.

'Kids! Go!' I yelled, and we began to crawl fast toward the doors. I had no idea how we'd get them open.

As it turned out, Mother Nature helped us. Sort of. Sort of a half-helped/half-killed situation. When we were about seven feet from the doors, they blew open, their frames shattering around the massive locks. In an instant, we were airborne, without using our wings.

The wind coming through the windows and whipping out through the doors created a huge updraft that almost flattened us against the ceiling. Gozen hunkered down over the UD even as a large potted plant clocked him in the head, opening the skin to reveal tissue and wires. Yes. Gross.

There was only one thing to do.

'Go with the flow!' I shouted, remembering a long-ago lesson from the Voice. 'Go with nature! Fang! Get Akila!' I grabbed Total and clutched him hard against my chest. I saw Fang grab Akila and knew she would be a struggle to hold.

Then, making sure that everyone was with me, I put my wings out just a bit, and *whoosh!* The wind grabbed me, and I shot down the hall like a jet.

'Ouch! Ouch! God—' I couldn't aim, so I was scraping against exit signs and light fixtures. I checked behind me to make sure everyone had gotten out, and they had, with no sign of Gozen or the UD.

'Go with the flow!' I yelled again. Then I saw where the hallway led: directly to a balcony with floor-to-ceiling windows. Of hurricane-proof glass. That we'd probably smash against like mosquitoes against a windshield.

'Wait! I take it back! *Don't go with the flow!*' I shrieked, trying desperately to backpedal.

But of course it was too late by then.

CHAPTER SIXTY-NINE

I hoped the Uber-Director hadn't paid his building contractor yet, because those so-called hurricane-proof windows were, in fact, not at all hurricane proof. Unless maybe for a baby hurricane. A widdle one. With no big winds. I thought he should have got his money back.

Instead of smashing against the balcony windows, we sailed *through* them, because they'd blown out by the time we reached them. Wastebaskets, plants, chairs, and even some desks flew out around us. Then it was like we'd been put into God's washing machine, on the spin cycle. I held on to Total as tight as I could, and we were sucked away into winds stronger than anything I'd ever experienced. My breath was actually pulled from my lungs. Within seconds, Total and I were soaked. In addition to the rain, hailstones as hard as diamonds pelted me, feeling like needles being driven into my skin. I pulled my wings in almost all the way, leaving them out a tiny bit in the hopes that this would allow me to steer. If I'd put them out fully, they would have been torn off.

When I looked back, I counted five bird kids behind me, all struggling. Fang and Iggy were both holding on to Akila. Nudge, Gazzy, and Angel had tied themselves together, ropes looped around their waists, which was smart, but I bet it really hurt.

'This sucks!' Total yelled in my ear.

I didn't think that needed a response. It was the understatement of the century. But come to think of it, I couldn't believe we were still alive. We weren't supposed to be able to survive this. No one could. Were we getting stronger? I started to wonder, then realized there was still time to be shredded to pieces.

Feeling almost half delirious from lack of breath, certain that my skin was being peeled slowly from my face and hands, I started expecting to see Dorothy's house swirling by at any moment—and then suddenly it was much calmer, and I was being sucked downward, fast.

My ears rang with silence. My mouth dropped open in surprise. I looked up and saw . . . white clouds and blue sky. It wasn't raining or hailing on me. I was still moving in a gigantic circle, but it was more like the fluff 'n' dry cycle, not too bad.

'We're falling,' Total told me.

Ah, yes, so we were. Cautiously I put my wings out more fully, feeling wind catch in them, expanding my feathers. I surged upward and saw my flock pop out of the wall of clouds one by one.

'We're in the eye of the storm!' I shouted, and motioned downward. I didn't know how big this eye was—maybe several miles across? But I wanted to take advantage of it. Controlling my descent, I headed earthward, landing on a broken section of highway overpass. At each end, the high-way dipped down into floodwaters—who knew how deep?

Shading my eyes, I looked up to see Nudge, Gazzy, and Angel, beat up and exhausted, land clumsily. Angel fell to her knees, trying to protect her broken arm.

I rushed over to them, untied their rope, and checked them all over.

Iggy landed, then Fang.

217

'Where's—?' I began, then saw Fang's face. I glanced at Iggy; he had the same tragic expression. Akila had been too heavy for them. They hadn't been able to hold on to her.

My heart squeezed painfully. What would we tell Total? Right now he was flopped on his side, panting, but any second he would realize the love of his life was missing. . . . Oh, God.

'Gozen.'

My head whipped up and I looked where Fang was pointing. High, high above us, Gozen and, amazingly, the Uber-Director were flailing wildly by, close to the edge of the eye. Suddenly my fury overwhelmed me—at Akila's death, at Angel's broken arm, at their trying to sell us, and at every other bad thing that anyone had ever done to us, which, believe me, was a pretty long list. In seconds I was streaking upward as fast as I could.

CHAPTER SEVENTY

Gozen was wrapped around the Uber-Director, which was the only reason the UD hadn't come apart by now. But even as I shot toward them, I could see that Gozen's weight was working against him; they were both being dragged roughly around the eye wall of the storm.

I saw the UD shout, 'Don't let go!' though I couldn't hear him. But Gozen's enormous fingers were slipping, and his body and face bore signs of violent contact with a lot of debris.

Gozen's eyes met mine as I got close, blue lasers into brown. 'Help me,' he rumbled.

'I don't think so,' I said, kicking at his arm. That was all it took—me kicking his arm in retaliation for his breaking Angel's—and his hold on the UD collapsed and Gozen spun away, falling heavily downward, his face assuming the only expression he was capable of: horror.

I held on to the UD's wheelchair. Fluid was leaking from his boxes; his human eyes in his human face were terrified.

'I control more than you could ever realize,' he gasped. 'I can make you rich beyond your wildest dreams. I can protect you for the rest of your life. Just save me now.'

If he'd been a real person, I would have hesitated. I'm not a killer. I mean, not on purpose, anyway. But he was a machine, someone's consciousness hooked up to a bio-mechanical body.

Plus, he was a complete and total jerk.

'You need to not be in this world,' I told him, and let go.

I didn't watch, but I'm sure the boxes snapped grotesquely apart in the next instants, and that he whirled around in the storm in pieces for a while. I never saw any part of him again.

I negotiated my way out of the eye wall, glad to be free of the rain and hail again, and flew downward until I saw the flock a mile or so away. We needed to escape this hurricane before the next eye wall hit us. As I came to a landing, I could see them huddled around Total, who had collapsed, sobbing, on the ground. Angel had tears in her eyes as she stroked him with her good arm. His small black wings, still unusable but getting bigger every day, were fluttering pathetically.

I stood nearby, breathing hard, barely able to take in the fact that Gozen and the Uber-Director were no more. Poor Akila. Poor Total. I shook my head, feeling terrible for him.

Angel looked up. 'Akila,' she said, frowning.

I nodded. 'I know, sweetie. I'm so sorry.'

'No—*Akila,*' said Angel, pointing at the sky.

'Huh?' was all I had time to say before an eighty-pound Malamute plummeted out of the sky, smashing right into me and knocking me onto my not-nearly-padded-enough butt.

'Oh, God,' I wheezed, Akila's body lying heavily on top of me. For the second or third time that day—it was hard to keep track—I had to slowly suck in breath, looking like a largemouth bass. 'Akila!'

The others rushed over, and Fang pried open Akila's eyelids and put his head on her side to listen for a heartbeat.

'She's alive,' he said, just as the mud-spattered dog blinked weakly.

'Uh, can you get her off me?' I said, my voice muffled. I felt as though I'd been hit with a warm, sopping-wet, furry sack of cement.

'Akila!' Total cried, now that the shock was wearing off. 'Akila! I thought we had lost you forever!' Eagerly he licked her face. I was thinking *bleah*, but Akila seemed to like it, turning her head so Total could get her other side.

And there we were. Together again.

CHAPTER SEVENTY-ONE

We managed to stay inside the eye of the hurricane, moving with it until the storm had weakened enough for us to fly out. As we flew over the devastation, I realized at last the full implications of what global warming could mean for our world.

'You were right,' I said quietly to Fang as we flew. 'Global warming is something we have to help stop.'

'What was that?' Fang said loudly, cupping one hand around his ear. 'What did you say?

Could you repeat that?'

I looked at him sourly. 'So what now, hot stuff? I have to tell you, I'm not loving the idea of going back to Antarctica. That place was like living inside a big fridge.'

'I was thinking we'd get something to eat, then call Dr. Martinez,' he suggested.

I smiled at him, my first real smile in . . . I didn't know how long. 'An excellent notion.'

CHAPTER SEVENTY-TWO

Washington DC

'I'm gonna barf,' I whispered to Fang, wiping my sweaty hands on my jeans.

'You'll be fine,' he whispered back. 'You always are.'

'I'm gonna die,' I moaned.

'You can't die,' he said, a hint of a smile in his voice. 'You're the indestructible Max.'

'I've never faced anything this hard before.' Yes, I sounded like a pathetic weenie. I prefer to think of it as showing my softer side.

'Max?' My mom stood at the door, smiling at me. She was all dressed up and looked fabulous. I would be lucky if I grew up to look like her. Which I guess would be hindered by my refusal to girlify myself. I looked down at my clean T-shirt and jeans. Mom had thoughtfully supplied me with a nice actual dress, but when I'd tried it on, I felt—I don't know. Vulnerable? Like I couldn't move, couldn't fight.

Well, we all have issues.

At least my clothes were totally clean, though my T-shirt advertised Güero's Taco Bar in Austin, Texas. On top of that I wore my traditional oversize, loose Windbreaker, because why would I want Congress staring at my wings?

Yes. Congress. There, in a nutshell, was my whoopsy-daisy life: Many evil people wanted to kill me, or sell me, or use me for evil purposes, and on the other hand, there I was, testifying about global warming to the Congress of the United States. Sometimes the lines got a little blurry.

'Okay, do you have your notes?' Brigid Dwyer came up and brushed some lint off my jacket, as if that would help.

'Yep.' I held up my sheaf of paper. Brigid, Michael, and the other scientists from the *Wendy K.* had helped me come up with what to say. All except Brian. He'd turned out to be another mole for the UD. He was in jail. There's always one—or in this case two—in every crowd.

'I think they're ready for you,' my mom said, gesturing at the open door. I could hear the buzzing of voices inside and wished fervently that the Capitol Building had an open ceiling that I could escape through if necessary.

'This is your mission,' said Jeb, smiling at me. 'You're fulfilling your mission right now, right here.'

I nodded, took a deep breath, and gave one last look at my flock. They were lined up, scrubbed clean, looking awed and a little freaked. Angel waved at me, and I waved back.

Showtime, folks.

CHAPTER SEVENTY-THREE

My hands shook. The microphone in front of me seemed too big, and I'd made it squeak by getting too close. I wished I could just beat someone up and get the heck out of here.

I cleared my throat and looked down at my speech.

'Thank you for inviting me here today,' I said, my voice sounding nothing like me. 'I'm here to testify about things I've seen and experienced myself. I'm here because the human race has become more powerful than ever. We've gone to the moon. Our crops resist diseases and pests. We can stop and restart a human heart. And we've harvested vast amounts of energy for everything from night-lights to enormous superjets. We've even created new kinds of people, like me.

'But everything mankind'—I frowned—'personkind has accomplished has had a price. One that we're all gonna have to pay.'

I heard coughing and shifting in the audience. I looked down at my notes, and all the little black words blurred together on the page. I just could not get through this.

I put the speech down, picked up the microphone, and came out from behind the podium.

'Look,' I said. 'There's a lot of official stuff I could quote and put up on the screen with PowerPoint. But what you need to know, what the world needs to know, is that we're really destroying the earth in a bigger and more catastrophic way than anyone has ever imagined.

'I mean, I've seen a lot of the world, the only world we have. There are so many awesome, beautiful things in it. Waterfalls and mountains, thermal pools surrounded by ice and snow as far as you can see. Beautiful beaches with sand like white sugar. Fields and fields of wildflowers. Places where the ocean crashes up against a mountainside, like it's done for hundreds of thousands of years.

'I've also seen concrete cities with hardly any green. And rivers whose pretty rainbow surfaces came from an oil leak upstream.

Animals are becoming extinct right now, in my lifetime. Just recently, I went through one of the worst hurricanes ever recorded. It was a whole lot worse because of huge, worldwide climatic changes caused by . . . us. We, the people.'

I suddenly remembered a catchy (if annoying) song I'd heard over and over in a Saturday morning cartoon—the one that was supposed to teach kids about the Constitution. The words of the preamble, which were quoted in the song, came flooding back to me. "We the People of the United States,"' I began, "in Order to form a more perfect Union, establish Justice, insure domestic Tranquility, provide for the common defence, promote the general Welfare, and secure the Blessings of Liberty to ourselves and our Posterity, do ordain and establish this Constitution for the United States of America."'

The room was silent. I looked around at all the faces. 'A more perfect union? While huge corporations do whatever they want to whoever they want, and other people live in subway tunnels? Where's the justice of that? Kids right here in America go to bed hungry every night, while other people get four-hundred-dollar haircuts. Promote the general welfare? Where's the general welfare of strip-mining, toxic pesticides, industrial solvents

226

being dumped into rivers, killing everything? Domestic tranquility? Ever sleep in a forest that's being clear-cut? You'd be hearing chain saws in your head for weeks. The blessings of liberty? Yes. I'm using one of the blessings of liberty right now, my freedom of speech, to tell you guys, who make the laws, that the very ground you stand on, the house you live in, the children you tuck in at night, are all in immediate, catastrophic danger.'

I took a deep breath, really getting warmed up. The flock was standing all around me, and Mom and Jeb were off to one side. I glanced at Mom, and she looked so proud. I hoped that Angel wasn't turning into a bird of paradise, and that Nudge wasn't making pens fly toward her. And if there was a God, Gazzy would not demonstrate his new skill right here in Congress.

'Every minute of every day, cars belch exhaust. Factories spew toxins into the air, land, and water. We've cleared millions of square miles of forests, rain forests, and plains, which means tons of topsoil is just washing away. Which means loss of animals and plants, and increased fires, floods, and coastal disintegration. Just by stuff people have made, created, we're raising the overall temperature of the entire atmosphere. Well, we only have the one atmosphere! What do you plan to do when it's destroyed? Can we all hold our breath until we get a new one?'

No one shouted out an answer.

'The problem is here, *now*,' I went on. 'Nine of the ten hottest years ever recorded have happened in my lifetime. I'm fourteen. More or less. There have been record-setting weather extremes across the globe— tornadoes, hurricanes, typhoons, droughts, wildfires, tsunamis. We're warming up the planet, and the planet's ice is melting. If only *fifty percent* of the world's ice melts, countless rivers and streams will overflow and then dry up, killing hundreds of thousands of people from disease and starvation. The ocean water level will rise anywhere from four feet to maybe twenty feet. How many of your favorite vacation spots would be under water? Want to see the Eiffel Tower by canoe? Do any of you own beach houses? Kiss 'em good-bye. And not two hundred years from now. Soon. Maybe within this lifetime.'

I swallowed and wished I had like an Icee or something. 'We can't reverse this disaster, even if we all pitched in now and did everything we could, which, face it, we're not going to do. A small percentage of us will do stuff, and other people will ignore the problem and hope they'll be dead before it gets really bad. But there are things we can do that would at least help. It would make a difference.

'The US could ratify the Kyoto treaty. Pretty

much every country in the world, except us and Australia, has ratified it. How can we be so pigheaded? Wait—don't answer that. I know our time here is limited.

'In general, we need to pay more attention to what we do, what we buy, who we buy it from. Use compact fluorescent bulbs. If every house in America replaced just *one* of its regular lightbulbs with a compact fluorescent, it would be like taking a million cars off the road. I mean, how hard is that? I can do the math, and I've never even gone to school!

'Look into other kinds of power. Windmills, water mills, solar power—every year corporations pay a jillion dollars in legal fees to avoid getting fined for pollution violations. What if they took a tiny percentage of that money and put it toward coming up with better energy sources?

'Right now America looks like a fatheaded, shortsighted, gas-guzzling, arrogant blowhard to the rest of the world. And Sweden looks all clean and tidy and progressive. I mean, where's our sense of pride?

'Why can't *we* be the progressive leaders, showing the rest of the world how to clean up its act? Why can't we, *the people,* get more involved and push through legislation that will help clean up our air, land, and water? Why can't we take government funds from stupid things like war and use them for programs that will develop better fuel sources?

'I'm just one kid, and not even a regular kid. But if I can come up with all this, why can't you? Will you wait until the water is lapping at your feet?'

I stopped abruptly. To tell you the truth, I could have gone on and on. I could have kept them pinned in their chairs all day while I recited facts and figures. But I hoped that at least a little of what I had said would stick, and make them think.

That was all I could do to save the world.

Epilogue

HOW BAD CAN IT BE?

CHAPTER SEVENTY-FOUR

'Gee, a fancy school in northern Virginia,' Iggy muttered. 'How bad can it be?'

'I'm sure nothing disastrous or life threatening will happen to us while we're here,' I said, sounding much more gullible than I am.

Here we were at Ye Olde Academy for Mutants and Other Kids. Shortly after my Oscar-worthy speech to Congress, my mom had explained that some important people had gone ahead and created a school for us. Frankly, we'd all been ready to kick back and relax on a non-hurricaned beach for a while, but Mom and Jeb had asked us to give the school a try. So here we were.

It was the ribbon-cutting ceremony, and when I'd taken a gander at the government limos, bigwigs, news teams, and stuff, I'd cottoned on to the fact that this was a big deal.

Plus, my mom; my half sister, Ella; Jeb; and some of the scientists from the *Wendy K.* were all there, beaming at us. I don't know who had created this school (actually called the Lerner School for Gifted Children—I thought they'd misspelled *Learner,* but then found out Lerner was some guy who donated a bunch of money), and I had no idea why anyone who knew us would think that we'd be here for any length of time, but hey! I was willing to try anything once!

So here we were, my flock. Angel's arm was all better, Akila had fully recovered (but still weighed eighty pounds, which still posed a humongo problem carting her furry butt around when we flew), Total's wings had continued to grow, and yesterday he'd gotten his two front paws about an inch off the ground. I almost missed Antarctica—not the coldness part but the empty cleanness of it, and the fact that we'd been relatively safe there (until we were captured, anyway), and the meaning of the work we'd done there. I missed the penguins. The leopard seals? Not so much.

We were all clean, and I only mention this because it was something new and different. Cameras were flashing all around us. Our former 'lie low and be anonymous' rule was pretty much shot all to heck. I'd had a great visit with my mom and Ella, and do not tell anyone I said this, but I was relieved that Brigid was staying in Antarctica and Fang was staying here.

I wondered if they had rounded up some of the other mutant kids I'd crossed paths with at the Institute and at Itex. I had always felt kinda sorry for them. They seemed lonely, like they didn't have a flock, or a family, or a purpose in life.

'And now, without further ado, I give you the Lerner School for Gifted Children!' The mayor of this small town stepped forward and cut the ribbon across the front entrance with a big pair of scissors that wouldn't be good for anything except stuff like this. The wide ribbon fell neatly apart, and everyone clapped and took pictures.

Max?

I didn't pay any attention for a moment, and then I realized that it was actually my Voice, the one inside my head. (I wonder if that phrase will ever sound less weird.)

What? I thought.

I know you're in the middle of something here, and I hate to interrupt, but there's another mission for you.

Huuuh? What are you talking about? I just did my mission! And almost died! A bunch of times!

Max, Max, Max, said the Voice in that irritating way it had. *The world isn't saved yet, is it? You've got work to do. Now, get out of there, and I'll give you the coordinates of where you need to go.*

Well. I weighed some unknown, probably difficult, possibly deadly mission, with us not knowing where we were going or what we'd be doing, against this bright, shiny new school building, no doubt full of gleaming desks and

235

Macs everywhere.

Never let it be said that I, Maximum Ride, would ever shirk my duty.

'Come on, guys,' I said to the flock. 'Gotta go. More world to save. All this book learning's going to have to wait.'

Nudge looked relieved, and Gazzy said, 'Oh, thank God.'

'Max?' said my mom.

I gave her a quick hug and a kiss, and Ella too.

'Duty calls,' I said. 'I'll let you know where I am. Thanks for everything.'

'I love you,' she said, because she's the coolest mom in the entire messed-up world.

Many cameras went off when the six of us, holding Total and Akila, whom I now thought of as the world's heaviest Malamute, took running starts, unfurled our wings, and soared into the sky, just like that.

My heart was so full of freedom that I felt like it might burst.